The Workhouse Waif's Remedy

BERYL WHITE

ROMANCE
PUBLISHING

COPYRIGHT

Title: The Workhouse Waif's Remedy

First published in 2021

ISBN: 9798477874675 (Print)

Copyright © 2021 Beryl White

CONTENTS

1

THE VIEW FROM THE WINDOW

In her rainy Whitechapel courtyard, Mabel Nithercott fought to get the washing in, the tenement building's soot-blackened bricks enclosing her in the squalid little space. Her left forearm ached as it clutched a bundle of sopping wet washing into her chest. Blindly, her fingers grasped the air in front of her, hunting for another garment to unpeg.

"Need help getting that in?" asked elderly neighbour Mrs Kirkham, each word wagging the cigarette in the corner of her mouth.

"Thanks. You're all right, Lydia. I'll manage," mumbled Mabel, her face now buried in the folds of fabric.

The muddy floor squelched with each step as she made her way along the washing line. The stair-rod like rain glued her hair onto her forehead and cheeks. Despite experimenting with the labour-saving laundry equipment at Whitechapel's new public baths and washrooms, her household chores had not gone well that day. The drudgery was as laborious as ever.

"How's things, Mabel? Getting back to normal yet, after, you know—?"

"—Not really. I'm managing, but ma's still a wreck. We'll get through it. People always do."

Lydia gave a compassionate smile and nodded. Mabel vanished down the alley and off to the two small rooms her cheek-by-jowl family called home. Then, kicking the door open, the girl staggered to the dining room and dropped the clothing in a soggy heap.

With the washing safely out of the terrible weather, she stretched their spare washing line across the claustrophobic little room, pegging out the clothes as best she could. Earlier, at the wash house, she could barely keep her eyes open and her mind on the job. She forgot to check the condition of the fabrics before pummelling them with the heavy dolly. The tiny tear in her father's best white work shirt deteriorated into a long rip she only noticed now. Her cash-strapped father, Joe, would be furious. East End families like the Nithercotts couldn't afford patched second-hand clothes, let alone new.

The damp air in their chilly home made her wheeze and cough. The last thing the family needed was more mold to contend with, but there was nowhere else to dry the laundry. With the clothes dripping above her, she returned to the remaining chores for the day. She had been delighted to start her first proper job as a draper's assistant in Spitalfields only a month before. How she longed to be there again, but it was not to be. Her sister's problems had cruelly slammed the door on that opportunity.

With bitter regret, she had complied with her parents' wishes to leave. They had their reasons for the decision, good reasons, but it didn't make the sudden loss any more palatable. The job had been the one thing that got her away from her suffocating home life and gave her hope for a brighter—independent—future. Despite a rough start in life, her teachers considered her a creative and intellectually gifted child. Sadly, household drudgery meant she no longer had an outlet for those talents. The daily grind was her only option—for now.

She peeled some wizened vegetables and piled them on top of a pig's trotter lying in their only cast-iron pan, then topped it up with water and a big handful of salt. Grizzling, she snatched the poker and jabbed at the dwindling red embers in the range. Coal was a luxury that the Nithercotts could ill afford. Hopefully, there would be just enough heat left to make the meal.

'Lord, what did I do to deserve this?'

2

UNEXPECTED NEWS

It was understandable to pull Mabel out of work, even if it worsened the family's bickering. Her parents were the only consistent breadwinners, and all the children were a constant drain on their finances. They were entitled to expect their offspring to contribute labour rather than cold, hard cash. The choice was stark: the mother and father could continue to work to line their greedy landlord's pockets with rent money, or they would all be sent to the workhouse. Mostly paid in 'experience', an apprentice's remuneration paled into insignificance compared to what her parents could earn on a good day. Alas, 'good days' at the market took a punishing amount of effort and, thus, no one was left to do the chores. It was simple. Mabel's hands were needed for necessary housework, so Ruth could maximise her time spent hawking. The floor may have been swept spotlessly clean, but the dripping laundry had ruined her efforts to make the tenement more welcoming. The small, drab range gave off a cheery orange glow, but not nearly enough heat to dry out the puddles on the flagstones.

Moving on to the next chore on her mother's list, she began cleaning the filthy sash windows, not that there was much to see outside. It lets more light in, she supposed. Huffing and puffing, she scrunched a piece of newspaper into a ball, then splattered it with malt vinegar. Making her way from top left to bottom right, each of the small panes was breathed on then thoroughly buffed. There was one thing in the Nithercotts' favour: their windows were still fully glazed. Many of their neighbours had draughty smashed panes, loosely filled with sack cloth or paper. As she scrubbed at a stubborn bit, she heard voices in the street. Peering through the freshly cleaned peep hole, she noticed burly publican, Fergus O'Brien, and his bouncer, Hook-Handed Alf, turfing out a couple of drunken labourers. Clearly, the sailors had been in The Little Drummer Boy since their night shift had ended hours ago, their increasingly raucous custom no longer welcome. Sprawled on the cobbles, the two out-of-towners yelled at the indignity of it all. Furious, Fergus gave as good as he got.

"I don't want to see you feckin' lads back
here till you've sobered up. No one talks to
my regulars like that! Got it?"

In retaliation, the men staggered to their feet and muttered curses as they bobbed and weaved towards the Red Lion on Dean Street, a local dive they knew would gladly take anyone's money regardless of the state they were in. As Mabel watched them wobble round the corner, her keen eye noticed a rag-ged-looking couple wending their way up the narrow lane. Her face fell.

The woman was her cake-hawking mother, Ruth. A wet grey shawl enveloped her upper body. A pitiful defence against the biting wind and rain, her left hand pulled the fabric close to her belly. The exposed right hand steadied a large wooden hawking tray hanging in front of her. The trudge back from the Ex-mouth Street market had been long and tedious. The tray banged into her bony hips with each step. The sisal strap rubbed her neck red raw. Tired and hun-gry, she stooped with the strain, both mental and physical. Unable to see her feet beneath the tray, she did her best to ignore the sludge oozing through the holes in her battered leather boots or to trip over her mud-caked hemline. A black hat tied with a fraying ribbon kept the rain off her face—if the brim wasn't bent back by the bracing headwind.

Her husband shivered beside her, desperately in need of a proper winter coat. His empty barrow, painted with bright signage advertising 'Nithercott's Fine Cat Meat,' bumped along the higgledy-piggledy cobbles. Like all sellers in his line of work, Joe wore a plush and distinctive black velvet waistcoat over his white shirt, though the pristine collars and cuffs were showing dirt after a few days of wear.

A proud, hardworking man, the thought of putting on a freshly laundered shirt tomorrow put a spring in his step. In the meantime, a blue-and-white spotted handkerchief helped cover the grime between washes. A crisply starched blue apron and black corduroy trousers completed his ensemble. The soaked garb clung to his gaunt frame like wet bunting to a pole, making him look forward to picking up his winter coat from the pawnbrokers—providing they had a few good days' sales beforehand. Profits had been elusive of late. This year, his overcoat had spent more weeks in the pawnshop than out.

Despite the grim weather, the street was crowded with people sheltering under doorway arches. The women gossiped as the men nipped from one dry alcove to the next, pulling their coat collars up around their ears. Young Gerry McGinty was bringing in the last of the stock at the chandler's shop on the corner. If he let the rain ruin any of the merchandise, his uncle Jimmy would give him a good thrashing. A few scrawny dogs and some tormented hens ran amok, chased by boisterous children delighting in grabbing their tails. Oblivious, the excited kids slammed into Joe and Ruth, offering no hint of an apology. The hunched, shambling figures looked desperate because they were.

Mabel darted towards the heavy black kettle and manoeuvred it onto the hottest part of the stove. After a long day, a hot drink was always welcome. When she looked up the lane again, she saw her parents still marching home in determined silence. There was no denying that hawking was a tough life, but it was the only option as unskilled workers. A gust of wind whipped the edges of Ruth's shawl from her numbed fingers, revealing a rotund belly. Heavy with child, her abdomen protruded over her empty hawker tray. She grimaced and drew the material around her to cocoon herself once more. Mabel pondered their unexpected early arrival. Maybe they've had a good day and sold everything already? Heaven knows we need the cash! The relentless regularity of their landlord's visit demanding the weekly rent could have set a station clock. Clemency was not his strong suit if families fell on hard times. Exhausted and relieved, Joe ploughed his cart into the front door so forcibly that the handle smacked into the wall, leaving a dent in the plaster. Perhaps his rage about the endless daily grind not improving their circumstances getting the better of him, or perhaps it was just a struggle to navigate the threshold with the cart.

"Just once, could you watch what you're doing!"

Ruth's nagging fell on deaf ears. Joe parked his cart in the front room, and he snatched Ruth's tray. The rope strap yanked her head forward as it caught on her bonnet. With a loud clatter, the tray landed on the barrow. The noise startled the bump in the mother's belly. The bulge screamed, for the child was no longer a foetus but a three-month-old infant—a baby brother, Billy, strapped to his mother for 'safekeeping' as she worked. Ruth loosened the ties and dumped the screaming, swaddled child onto the tiny dining table. Fiery-eyed, Joe stood with his hands on his hips, seething. Mabel tried her hand at peace-keeping.

"How about a nice cup of tea, eh? Warm your cockles up?"

The kind offer was met with silence, the marital acrimony too bitter to be sweetened with a mere cuppa. Despite being ignored, she made the drinks, preferring to be needlessly busy than helpless.

"It wasn't my fault, Joe!"

"Fiddlesticks! Thanks to your selfishness, we had to cut the day short! Now we're potless. Mabel should look after Billy, but you just won't let her, will you? Why can't you accept lightning won't strike us twice?"

By her sides, Ruth let her fists relax—it made slapping Joe's face easier. He rubbed the rosy, stinging patch on his cheek then raised his hand to retaliate, but his conscience thought better of it.

On the table, the tiny open-mouthed little figure continued to add to the tremendous ruckus in the room. Wrapped up, mummified in grim white bandages, all Billy could do was pivot his head about his neck and yell. Irritable and hungry, the poor mite shrieked at the top of his lungs. Despite the obvious distress he was in, the Nithercotts accepted his incarceration was done with kindness, not malice. Too angry to take care of their son, the parents assumed Mabel would add another chore to her growing list. Again, the obedient girl obliged.

Cooing as she picked up Billy, she let his fuzz-covered head rest in the crook of her arm, then struggled to navigate up the narrow creaky stairs. One of the lower treads had suddenly given way under someone's foot a month ago, leaving a treacherous gap to negotiate. She laid the lad on the coarse grey bedspread. Trussing up the tot so tightly might have seemed cruel to an onlooker, but it was vital to his wellbeing. Teasing away the bandages, the further in she got, the more yellowy things became, stained by a mass of weeping sores that covered the infant's lower limbs. The lack of fresh air had weakened his skin terribly.

Now freed, Billy's grotesque clubbed feet began to thrash about. Badly bowed, his lower legs looked more curved than an umbrella handle, forming a distinct inward 'j' shape from his shins downwards. His misshapen tendons made each tiny toe overlap its contorted neighbour. Stretching his ligaments into proper alignment was the only way walking in later life would be possible.

The street's gossips soon spread the word about Billy's cruel deformity. A week after his birth, Ruth chatted with her nosy neighbour, Milly Compton, in the corner shop. Milly mentioned that when she was dusting at her employer's house, she had overheard her boss talk of a new technique that could cure club-foot. The process, the brainchild of a Bloomsbury hospital surgeon, had been described in a newspaper article, so she said. At first, Ruth dismissed the idea thinking the treatment would be beyond their financial means, but after discovering how simple it was, she attempted the procedure herself.

Several times a day, the mother repeatedly massaged his feet to lengthen the tendons, followed by the application of strong bandages to maintain the correction. The hope was that if treatment began early before the deformity of the bones was well-established, the leg tissue would lengthen within two to three months of birth. Luckily for Ruth, Mrs Kirkham helped get the muslin to tie around the young lad's limbs.

"It has to work, Lydia. It just has to."

The old woman was all too aware of the consequences if the treatment failed—Billy would be crippled for life. Earning a wage to support himself would be impossible. Life was tough enough for the able-bodied Nithercotts, without debilitation to contend with. Ruth felt utterly compelled to try—whatever the odds, but when she was too exhausted, the massage duties fell into Mabel's lap.

He'd always looked scrawny since birth, but his weight had plummeted further in recent weeks. There was no interest in suckling whatsoever. He even refused to be hand-fed bone broth, preferring to writhe and wriggle his head away from the spoon. Pain and frustration overtook his instinct to eat. Feeding her son was getting increasingly problematic, but after a string of miscarriages, Ruth wasn't prepared to give up on him while he had breath in his body. Secretly, Joe wished she would.

No matter how gentle Mabel was, her brother's distress was palpable. Navigating his care regimen had become a moral minefield for the family. Did they continue to truss him up for most of the day to stop him becoming a cripple despite the sores? Did they remove the bandages until his skin healed but risk his soft bones permanently setting out of alignment? Or did they risk starvation taking him?

Despite the cruel gossip, other folk in their community pulled together to support the Nithercotts. Friends and neighbours listened to their concerns and popped round with another idea to try. Even Harry, Lydia Kirkham's errant son, had surprised them all by popping in with a (stolen) tube of a fashionable ointment used at his boss's workshop. Should one of the joiners have a mishap with a chisel, the gaffer swore blind the balm speeded up their recovery from any cuts and grazes. Cornelius Quimby's Cure-All Embrocation was causing quite a sensation in Britain, some even said worldwide. Posters at railway stations and quarter-page newspaper adverts extolled its efficacy. The promotions claimed the balm was nothing short of a miracle for a myriad of external ailments.

Harry's tin of Quimby's embrocation gave the Nithercott's a very precious gift—hope. For Billy, sadly, the ointment was anything but miraculous. There had been no improvement in days, despite following the instructions supplied to the letter—liberal and regular application thrice daily. Instead, the family opted for a homemade salve for his sores, based on a traditional recipe Lydia and Mabel concocted. Over time, it seemed to offer some relief against further infection.

Before moving to London, Mrs Kirkham had grown up in rural Essex. Country living had given her the practical knowledge of many health-giving plants growing in hedgerows, meadows, marshes, and woodland. One afternoon, Lydia and Harry had taken the train out towards Southend and gathered what the wise old woman needed to make the curious balm. The following day, in the Kirkham's tiny kitchen, Lydia jotted down the basic recipe. Together, she and Mabel boiled up the ingredients and decanted them into repurposed shoe polish tins. The small tins also doubled as handy dispensing tubs too. They made several batches. Mabel thought she knew the steps so well, she could make the salve in her sleep.

Upstairs in the family bedroom, as Mabel cared for Billy, the girl's ears picked up on her parents' protestations. The seventeen-year-old let them wash over her. Privacy was a luxury the Nithercott's could not afford. With a family of five crammed into such a small dwelling, she had mastered the art of selective deafness long ago, learning it was best to keep out of the way until the shouting had fizzled out. Her father's temper was seldom suitable for taming.

Mabel took the babe in her arms and rubbed on a thick layer of the unctuous ointment, then began manipulating his lubricated limbs. Faking a broad smile, tickling his chin every now and then, she managed to calm the boy. Exhausted, his little eyelids fluttered closed as she gently rocked him in her arms.

"Shush now, little one. Time for sleep," she whispered.

Moments later, Billy had his second wind and was back to thrashing about. It was bedlam. She bounced the lad above her head, rubbing noses with him, trying to keep his mood brighter. Finally, she noticed a frosty silence had returned to the front-room of number six, only interrupted by two empty enamel mugs clattering back on the range. She suspected it was safe to venture down once her brother had taken some bone broth.

The young girl reached for the cold cup of beefy liquid, the metal spoon grinding as she scooped up each morsel. Then, patiently, she offered his lips the nourishment, relieved to see Billy managed to gulp down several good mouthfuls of broth—before giving up in protest and locking his jaw firmly shut. Like that is it, Sonny Jim? I'll try again later, young man. You're not getting out of it that easily.

She lowered young Billy into the bottom drawer of the Nithercott's rickety bedside cabinet, wrapping him up tightly in a bedsheet, bunching up the spare fabric beneath him to form a basic mattress. A label sewn onto it read, 'The Deserving Woman's Christian Mission,' a venture set up by local temperance movement luminary Reverend Simeon Bennett. Mabel wasn't quite sure of its provenance but suspected the light fingers of Harry Kirkham might have had a hand in its acquisition.

The giggly infant gave Mabel a little gummy grin. This time, she replied with a genuine smile as she stroked his hollow cheek. His tiny hand wobbled up to grab her little finger and latched on like a limpet. It warmed her heart to see her brother calm after so much anguish earlier. She hoped her ma would note his improvement. 'I swear I am good at caring for him' she concluded correctly.

Billy began to snooze. She closed the drawer as much as she dared to stop her brother from rolling out and doing himself a mischief. Rest little one, rest. Mabel cooed as his eyes fluttered closed again.

> "We'll soon have you right as rain. This ointment of mine, well, it might whiff of paraffin and witch hazel, but it seems to be doing you some good."

Exhausted, the lad's little eyelids finally slid down to a close. As she looked at him, the worry about his future took hold again.

'Who wanted a cripple working for them? No one. That's who.'

3

UNEASY PEACE

Joe and Ruth were slumped at the dining table, staring out of the half-cleaned windows. Ruth's eyes were glazed over, but Joe's gaze went further, focusing on the warm lights adorning The Little Drummer Boy's golden interior. Like everyone else in Whitechapel, the temptation for the world-weary to drink their problems away was ever-present. Most of the time, the Nithercotts managed to ignore temptation, preferring to enjoy an occasional tipple to regular blind drunkenness. An early start with a blinding hangover was never pleasant.

The boozer was popular with the locals and the labourers passing through the area. At weekends, the landlord, Fergus O'Brien, often booked a musician to bash out a tune on the battered upright piano, something the cheaper spit-and-sawdust places didn't offer. The camaraderie and ambience that came with singing along to the music hall favourites of the day were welcome relief from the everyday grind for the working class. It provided a tiny oasis of relaxation in an otherwise brutal, impoverished, and hectic week—on a street that seemed to be attracting more and more undesirables as the years dragged by. If you were lucky enough to be in Jimmy McGinty's inner circle, in a hidden back room, you could also see bare-knuckle boxers batter each other to a bloodied pulp, away from the prying eyes of the law. The fearsome reputation of the dark tenements along Prospect Street made it an unofficial no-go area for the bobbies on their beats.

The affluent days of the wealthy Huguenot weavers were long gone. Their large townhouses with their tall windows had been sliced and diced into smaller and smaller weekly rents. The practice suited McGinty perfectly—the government's rules for landlords offering accommodation by the week were much more relaxed than longer monthly contracts. The underclass loved them too; the lax record-keeping and the police's unwillingness to venture into the poorest slums made it easy for a rogue to get away with murder—usually figuratively, sometimes literally.

The pub was a godsend when the Nithercott's twin girls were younger. Mrs Kirkham would step in to mind them in return for one of Ruth's unsold rock cakes. Then, if there was ever a problem at home, she could be over and summon them back in a flash. Usually, things went smoothly, and the couple got a brief break from the grind of parenthood and poverty. Through the pub's large bay window, Joe saw a couple of youths he recognised, cousins that worked for his cat meat supplier. They were laughing and joking without a care in the world.

That week, Joe knew frittering away any of their money on gin or ale was not the answer. Pawning his beloved overcoat was an option in the summer, but as the long winter months closed in, being without it was a cold, cruel blow to his wellbeing.

Mabel tiptoed downstairs, second-guessing what all the fuss was about this time. They've probably run into a busybody bobby down the market. They're always moving the costers on from their pitches on those narrow lanes. Maybe there just wasn't space? The notorious tangle of handcarts blocked the capital's transport arteries, causing havoc for goods distributors and people alike. Milly Compton said that one coster was so angry at being asked to move for the umpteenth time he tracked down the off-duty bobby and garrotted him. With reluctance, it was time for Mabel to get to the heart of her elders' angst. She played dumb, to begin with.

"So, you're back early, then? Sold all your stock?"

Her parents' heads turned from the window and the tempting lure of Friday-night freedom in The Little Drummer Boy.

"Yes. And no." hissed her cryptic father before grabbing a bottle of gin from the larder earmarked for 'emergencies'. "I'll let your mother explain."

There was a long pause as Ruth readied herself to speak. Looking at her daughter, she patted the wobbly chair next to her. Mabel dodged through the laundry and took a seat.

"Well—today—, we had to go to the charity hospital. It was Billy. His condition deteriorated in the wet weather. Been tipping it down all week, hasn't it? Must have got to him. I thought he was a goner. Lifeless like a rag-doll in my arms, he was. We needed to see the doctor immediately. We sold Joe's stock to Mick the Meat Man on the cheap and got Sam to take us on his cart. Gave him the last of my cakes for the fare."

"Cost us a pretty penny that little fiasco did. Easily avoided too to my mind," he complained, swigging at the gin again.

The burning liquor fully unleashed his harsh tongue, delivering a killer blow no mother should hear.

"It would have been better if the Lord had taken him at birth. He's not right, Ruth! Accept it. We've known he'd always be sickly ever since the midwife flinched when she pulled his twisted little body out of yours. Why God chose to spare him, I'll never know! He's got no future."

With red-rimmed eyes, Ruth bit her lip, but it wasn't enough to regain her composure. Mabel took a deep breath and stared at her father menacingly. Nothing.

"Well, pa? What happened?" she demanded.

"We'd had a good day, at first. Everyone wanted to buy from us. Even had a queue at one point," he explained. "Then, just after the lunchtime rush, your mother went off to a corner of the market to feed the little 'un while he seemed quiet. Pointless trying when he's yammering, yeah? Anyway, when she lifted her shawl, he didn't blink in the light or move. He was limp. She spoke to him and pinched his cheek good and proper, but there was nothing."

Ruth's fingers traced back and forth along the grain of the wood to distract herself from the truth. Deep down, she knew there was little chance of escape. A disabled child was a lifelong burden they could not afford. Joe continued. More of a realist, he said what his wife couldn't.

"At first, we thought Bill was cold or that perhaps he had tired himself out with all the screaming—he was a right little sod this morning. Next thing, I sees yer ma over by the wall, wailing over and over. 'I can't lose another nipper!' Everyone was staring at her as she tried to shake some life back into him, warm him up a bit. Didn't work, though, did it? Right bleedin' waste of time."

Ruth blinked hard. Mabel reached for her mother's hand and gave it a squeeze. Joe took another slug of gin.

"Well, she gave such a heart-wrenching cry, the other sellers looked at us wondering what to do, like. Although there was nothing they could do, of course—they ain't doctors, are they?"

"Then what?" asked Mabel as Ruth wrestled the gin off Joe.

"Well, the rain started coming down hard. Your mother was so shaken with the shock of it all she could barely walk. A few costers stepped up and offered to take the last of our stock off us. For once, the old rivalries were put aside. We didn't get the best price, but it did give us a bit of money and a ride. One of the lads with a donkey and cart came over, young Sam Whitmore. He offered to give us a ride home, but we chanced it and asked if he could take us to the hospital instead."

After a good hit of liquor, Ruth found her tongue.

"Bless Sammy for agreeing. He had to go well off his normal route. He could get the sack for that if Jimmy McGinty found he was using the work cart for his own unofficial errands."

Joe continued.

"Me and the lad yanked your mother and Billy on the cart like we were undertakers on a fresh pick up. The stress of it was all too much by now. Anyway, I leapt on the back to keep an eye on 'em as Sam geed up his donkey. Cor, the little tyke, went like a bull at a gate to get us there as quick as he could. Nearly ran over a few people in his haste. Shouted an apology over his shoulder as we clattered by. I half-expected peeling some coster up off the cobbles and throwing him on the back of the cart to come to the hospital with us."

He gave a shrug at the absurdity of it all. Ruth carried on.

"We had to wait a bit until we got to see one of the volunteer doctors. He had a look at Bill and warmed him up a bit, and thankfully the baby started to come around at last. But, crikey, the doctor gave our ears a chewing. Said the kid's in a terrible state, and he really needs some rest here at home. Clear his sores up a bit. But, o'course, he says he needs a damned good feed too. Said he looks like 'a bag of bones'."

Mabel nodded as her father took the gin again.

"Doc says we're to feed him up and take him back in a week for another consultation. Says he'll treat him for free. Took pity on us, he did. But he took a dim view of your mother taking him out hawking. He reckons if the infection gets any worse in this damp weather, well—it will see him off. 'Gotta look after him at home,' the doc warned. I said we could do that. Well—you could—Mabel."

An irate Ruth protested against the suggestion.

"It's not that simple though, is it, Joe? His legs need attention several times a day. Mabel's got her hands full looking after this place."

A defiant Ruth had no intention of changing. Her husband rolled his eyes in temper.

"I just need to keep him drier, and it will all work out. A few more weeks trussed up, a bit of Mabel's ointment, and he'll be sorted. That article said six months is all it takes to straighten bandy legs. We're over halfway there. He needs to be with me. I don't care what that posh doctor says. He only spent ten minutes with Billy. I know my own boy, Joe!"

He glared at her. Yes, dear. But that 'hoity-toity' doctor has trained with the surgeon who came up with the bleedin' treatment for clubfoot in the first place. All you've done is listen to some second-hand tittle-tattle from Milly bleedin' Compton.

"I'll borrow an oilskin from someone. That'll keep that rain off him."

"Of course, you will, Ruth. It's not like they'd need it for themselves in this weather, is it?"

"Alright then—the corner shop will have a bit of old sack cloth we can waterproof with some linseed oil. If he's warm, dry, and loved, he'll be fine."

Joe thumped the dining table with his thick meaty fists:

"Why do you have to be so stubborn, Ruth? You heard the doctor's warning."

Next door, Lydia Kirkham who vowed to drop off one of her oilskins later, could hear the yelling through the thin walls.   The raised voices woke Billy too, screeching in agony again. Livid, the two parents stared at each other, frozen, neither wanting to give in, both wanting their own way. Once more, it was left to their exasperated daughter to tend to the boy. Her feet thumped their way upstairs, frustrated that her mother's opinion of her caring abilities vacillated between utter reliance and grave doubts whenever it suited her.

The drawer creaked open as Billy was freed once more. Mabel cradled and rocked him until he settled again. He gave her a little smile as she spoon-fed him, and it melted her heart. She wanted what was best for Billy, even if it meant more struggle in her own life until he was stronger. Thinking better decisions would be made on his behalf if he were present. She headed for the front room, peering over the child's head as she descended, terrified of tripping down the treacherous hole. With her fleshy little nose hovering above his eyes, the boy's inquisitive fingers disappeared up her nostrils just as her foot was about to bridge the gap.

"Do you mind, mister! You had to do that then, didn't you, yer little horror."

Mabel ruffled his hair as the child began to chuckle again.

"I think that doctor's right, ma. Being stuck under a shawl in all weathers is no place for a poorly little 'un."

Ruth stood up. The chair clattered on the floor behind her.

"Well, I bet he's never had a kid die on him, has he? Not one of his own. A posh bloke's kids don't go wanting for much. What does he know about living from hand-to-mouth here?"

"I imagine quite a lot, Ruth, since the charity hospital is funded by the Tynedale Hall Philanthropic Society based here in Whitechapel."

Ruth snatched Billy off Mabel, adding:

"I'll keep an eye on him during the day. He'll be fine. Trust me."

The petulant mother stormed upstairs to attempt another feed to add weight to her side of the argument. Her furious voice boomed out.

"Mabel, why's he only had half a mug of broth since we got back? And people wonder why he's so bloody scrawny."

Bitter regret   filled Mabel's body once more. If her twin sister hadn't died suddenly three weeks ago, life would be very different for the Nithercotts. Her mother would have seen sense, been a little less overprotective, and stopped insisting Billy should be dragged out to the market in the harsh depths of winter. Swallowing repeatedly failed to dissolve the lump of guilt wedged in the girl's throat.

There was no need for Mabel to feel guilty about her sister. Esther's premature death had been no one's fault. Rather, it had been a terrible accident. The doctor in attendance had said so. But still, the unpleasant feeling of culpability lingered on for the one remaining twin. It happened when I was with her—so it must be my fault! In need of a distraction, Mabel pottered about the front room in a daze, jabbing at the runny stew with a spoon. Come on! Raking over the past won't bring her back!

Twenty minutes later, Ruth returned after another unsuccessful feed, a fact she kept secret by quaffing the last of the broth herself.

She set her son down in the frayed woven basket they kept beside the range, the warmest place in their draughty little home. No sooner had the child began to doze than Ruth pulled him from his slumber and gave him another slathering of the poultice and another rough manipulation, determined to prove she was best suited to the provision of care. Mabel and Joe looked on in despair as he was trussed up again for the night. They thought it was a wonder he could still breathe.

With her concerned ear pressed against the wall, Lydia noticed it was deathly quiet again.

Mabel dished up three portions of the watery stew, making sure her parents shared all the trotter meat between them. They ate in silence. Around them was the constant drip drip drip of the laundry, still no nearer to being dry and ready for the morning. Joe's shirt's grubby collars and cuffs would have to manage another day. The thought irritated him.

'It's about time someone did what I, Joe Nithercott wanted.'

4

DRUNKEN CONFESSIONS

As Mabel washed the pots, her drunken father was letting his nasty side loose. Sat silently, the two women knew he was simmering. His mind's eye had transformed the image of Billy's screaming mouth into a big black drain. Ruth was above it, gleefully shaking the last of the family's coins out of her purse. Chinking against the oily, ebony grate, the money tumbled out of sight, out of reach, into oblivion.

"Should have sssmothered him at birrth. Wouldn't be the firrsst parents to do it, " he huffed. "Plenty of unwanted kids end up at the bottom of the Regent's Canal in a sack, like an unexpected litter of kittens. If the midwife wasn't there, I would have done it myself there and then. He'll never be a normal lad, running down Prospect Street playing with his iron hoop and a stick. He'll be staring at them out of this bleedin' window, costing us bleedin' money."

When Joe's brain spun with drink, his cruel tongue took on a life of its own, his frustration tumbling out of him, one nasty word at a time.

"How dare you, Joe? You can be such a monster."

"No, I'm realistic! Unlike you! If he's not going in the canal, at least let Mabel look after 'im in the day for a week or two. Meet me halfway, eh?"

Ruth gave Joe a black look. It wasn't just Mabel who had regrets about Esther. Her mother blamed herself too. Going on that silly errand for a secondhand shirt was a mistake she would forever regret.

Many years earlier, they discovered one of their beloved girls was blighted with severe epilepsy. The family tried to control her violent and unpredictable fits, but it had proved difficult. Before heading out that fateful day, Ruth asked Mabel to take some food up to her sister and sit with her for a while. Poor Esther had gone to bed the night before, complaining of dizziness. Poor Esther had gone to bed the night before, complaining of dizziness. Esther was a home-loving girl who loved to take care of the family. Playful and caring, she was the one who always brightened their drab existence with her silly jokes and exuberant dancing.

For Mabel, the timing couldn't have been worse. She and Mrs Kirkham had planned to gather the ingredients for Billy's poultice. Lydia had grovelled for a few pennies from the neighbours to pay for the trip to Essex. There would be no more money forthcoming from the cash-strapped community for a second trip.

Carefully, quietly, Mabel tiptoed upstairs, carrying the plate of bread and dripping.

"Here you go. Ma's got you something nice and plain for lunch. You still feeling off?"

"A bit, but it's going. It's just hunger making me queasy, I think."

"Well, nibble on a bit of this. I'll come up and check up on you."

"Will you stop fussing, Mabel? I can eat on my own, or have you forgotten I'm seventeen too!"

"All right. Have it your way! I suppose that means you don't mind if I go out with Mrs Kirkham in half an hour?"

"Don't you mean 'go out with Harry?'"

"He'll be there—along with his mother," Mabel corrected.

"I reckon you've got a soft spot for that fella—admit it!" Esther said, giving her sister a cheeky wink.

"You can pack that in. But, if you must know, it's a working trip. We're looking for some special medicinal plants that Lydia says will help Billy."

"Calm down. I'm only pulling your leg. No need to be so defensive, Mabel."

Esther bit on the hunk of bread and chewed with a smile, then exaggerated swallowing it down.

"See? I'm eating! I'll be fine. You'd better get ready for Harry—I mean the train."

Mabel scuttled downstairs and waited for Mrs Kirkham to knock for her. Every time someone walked past her window, she jumped to attention, only to find it wasn't Lydia. In the end, she closed her eyes and had a quick doze at the dining table. Five minutes later, the young girl was startled by a loud knock at the door and two faces peering through the window at her. Harry mouthed: 'Time to go!'

"You two'd better come in. Just give me a minute, will you? I promised ma something."

"Be quick! Don't want to be late, do we?"

Mabel nipped upstairs to see if her twin wanted some more bread. At the top of the stairs, horrified, she saw Esther awkwardly contorted, her face blued, her wide eyes bulging out. She yelled as she shook her by the shoulder.

"Esther! Esther!"

Harry Kirkham bolted up towards the bedroom, nearly twisting his ankle as one of the lower stairs gave way under the heavy thump of his feet.

"She's not breathing, Harry! Do something!"

Mabel was hysterical, leaving the young man to assess the situation.

"Her throat. Something must be stuck in her throat!"

"The bread's gone down the wrong way!" Harry warned as he swept his finger in Esther's mouth.

With doctor's fees beyond the means of anyone in Prospect Street, it was time for the onlookers to get the cheapest help available.

"Ma! Something's not right with Esther. Fetch the chemist, now!"

Lydia Kirkham strode towards the nearest pharmacy, a small unit on Commercial Road, ignoring the pain from her arthritic knees and hips. The door crashed into the brass bell above with a deafening clang. The poor chemist's arms shot up in the air, spilling the tablets he was preparing all over his workbench.

"Madam! What do you think you're—"

"—6 Prospect Street. Quick. A girl is choking to death! Please help!"

With a life at stake, the stunned pharmacist ran like the wind, yelling over his shoulder:

"You stay here! Watch the shop."

Once in the little bedroom, the pained sadness on the young medic's face told everyone nothing more could be done. Placing her fingers lightly on Esther's eyelids, Mabel closed them. Harry put his hand on the distraught girl's shoulder and squeezed it tightly. For Mabel, his kind touch at such a heartbreaking time formed an unshakable bond. She didn't want him to ever let go, but let go, he did.

"No point us sitting here moping, Ma. What about the train?" said Harry.

The crass remark made Lydia give her son her trademark steely stare. Harry shrugged back at her.

"You go, Mrs Kirkham. I should tell my parents alone. It's for the best. And by Jove, poor Billy still needs help."

As the front door closed, wracked with guilt and sorrow, Mabel rehearsed how she would break the news. Despite her best efforts, it did not go well. The painful revelation crucified her mother, who laid the blame squarely at Mabel's feet. On the death certificate, the doctor put 'accidental death by asphyxiation during epileptic seizure.' Poor Esther had choked on her last meal.

Ruth blamed herself as much as Mabel for losing her precious daughter. The grieving mother berated herself. If only I'd stayed that day. Sat beside my Esther, chatting as she ate. She'd still be with us. All this pain because I went to see Bert the bleedin' Rag Man to patch Joe's tatty old overcoat. He can't even wear it because it's in the pawn shop window! For the mother and the sister, the grief and guilt were raw and savage.

As the wintery night drew on, back in the little front room, Mabel devoted her attention to making some fancy boxes for the corner shop. The packaging wasn't that fancy to look at, though, more functional than beautiful. Jimmy McGinty liked to buy his stock in bulk and sell it to his tenants in smaller quantities—at an extortionate price, of course. And woe betide anyone seen walking past his sentry-box of a shop with cheaper merchandise procured from further afield. No one on the street was surprised to discover the benefits of his shameless profiteering did not trickle down to his staff. Mabel earned a pittance, just one pitiful penny for one hundred boxes.

New to the fiddly activity, Mabel's production rate was poor, but she had to start somewhere and was determined to improve, whatever it took. With mastery, she hoped to earn enough to keep her father's overcoat out of Micky Pavlovich's premises. Hard-up households living hand-to-mouth usually worked together in the evening on such tasks, chatting, telling jokes and fireside stories, but not this family and definitely not tonight.

Working by candlelight put a terrible strain on her eyes, but she forced herself to continue. She counted the pile of finished pieces. Thirty boxes in two hours! Her jaw and stomach clenched as hard as iron. This is hopeless. Beside her, her gin-soaked father had fallen asleep, slumped over the table. After finishing the family's emergency liquor rations, he had gone to the Little Drummer Boy, after all, saying he had 'some urgent business to deal' with. He returned in quite a stupor. In the rocking chair by the range, Ruth was stabbing her cross-stitch embroidery with her trusty bodkin in hand, hoping it would release some pent-up aggression if she imagined stabbing at Joe and anything else that annoyed her. Mabel wasn't the only one at the end of her tether.

Close to midnight, Ruth and Joe finally retired for the night. Fearing Jimmy's wrath if she was late with his order, Mabel pushed on with the mountain of cheap cardboard to be folded until gone two o'clock. Then, exhausted, nerves jangling and fed up at the sight of a thin sliver of mattress, she shuffled into bed, hoping that neither her parents nor brother would awaken.

She lay there in physical discomfort, her mind whirring about what might happen to Billy tomorrow if Ruth dragged him out. Eventually the young girl joined them in their slumbers.

The next day, no one would be left guessing each of the Nithercott's family's fate.

5

GRIM NIGHT WORK

In another corner of the Parish of St Olave, Joe's main meat supplier was gearing up for a busy night. In the smoggy blackness, all four of Whitechapel's knackers' yards were now in full swing. Reliant on good old horse power to move people and the thousands of carts about the city streets, London had over a hundred old nags that needed to be disposed of each week. Everyone knew the beasts were a health hazard if they were left where they fell, but that wasn't the only motivation to deal with the corpses. Just as tending to live horses was a way to eke out a living, so too was dealing with dead and dying steeds. Thanks to the knackers grafting away on the grisly task, cat meat costers like Joe Nithercott could sell the freshly processed flesh in the morning. The process was so slick, the meat even had sufficient time to cook and cool before the dawn rush of sellers flooded into the yards. As gruesome professions went, flogging cat meat was a good choice because job security was sky-high. The word on the street was that cherished pets always needed feeding. Joe often joked that some daft old folk would put their silly cat's welfare before their own.

The capital had plenty of breweries, coal merchants and omnibus companies keen to offload a beast that was past its best—a dead horse outside the premises was not good for business. Collecting the carcasses was lucrative for the knacker's yard because, depending on its condition, an old horse could raise as much as two pounds. It was a good system all round.

Near the top end of Bishopsgate, cart lad Noah Sewell was two hours into his nightshift, making steady progress back to the knacker's yard with Stan, his trusty shire. The great horse strained to drag the high-sided wooden wagon behind him, laden with his dead equine brethren. Tonight, Noah prayed the straining leather straps held the bodies in place—the corpses were stacked five high. Dealing with the ones that fell en route was not pleasant. Behind the cart was his right-hand man and cousin, David, about to face his first shift in the grisly trade.

He had his hands full policing a string of five sickly nags, trooping behind the cart with a slow, unsteady gait, hoping that they all survived their final mile's walk. He dreaded to think how they would handle one popping its clogs on the way to the yard. The first nag was tied with a rope bridle to the back of the wagon. The others tied from tail to mouth, each following along placidly as if resigned to their fate. Noah didn't have the heart to tell David he had it easy that night, and on a busy shift, he might have to contend with fifteen.

Occasionally, one of the live horses would get a stay of execution, earning a reprieve because the yard's gaffer, Mr Gould, had a nose for spotting a specimen that could be turned around with a bit of covert, comfy stabling and a damned good feed. The young and wilder fillies and colts prone to biting and kicking could sometimes be broken and tamed then put to work delivering the yard's goods or hired to a local business—but that didn't happen often.

"Here, Noah, what if we rescued a horse on our rounds one day? We could buy it for fifteen shillings and sell it for a hundred or more? Think how many pints that would buy us down the Drummer Boy!"

"Are you mad, Davy? For one thing, if Mr Gould found out, he'd get Fred to flay you."

"Flay?"

"Don't worry, you'll find out. Besides, it's against the law. The authorities believe any horse destined for the knacker is to leave the yard as either processed meat or by-products—and nothing else."

"By-products?"

"Come on, we haven't got time to chat. We might have another round to do after this one."

"But there must be some that can be saved?"

Noah sighed then answered.

"Sometimes horses end up at Gould's because, like domestic servants, they fall out of favour with the household and get the chop. Then there's the favourite mount killed for throwing the rider, causing his master's untimely death. Maybe one that panicked and reared, injuring some posh fella's daughter. A mare that made her malicious mistress angry."

"And what about —"

"No more questions, David. Enough!"

In silence, the two lads trundled on into the cold night. Noah and Stan steered the load into the yard as David helped corral the live ones into place. Now, Fred Kemp's work could begin.

"Get one over here, lads. Ain't got all night."

The slaughterman needed to work speedily, not just to reduce the suffering but because stripping the bones of flesh took time. David untethered the tail-end horse and led it across to Fred's corner of the yard. Fred took the rope bridle and disappeared behind a large grubby tarpaulin strung from the roof. In a rare act of compassion, he had put it up to shield the impressionable young lads as he worked.

"Hello there, old boy", he whispered, patting the elderly horse on the neck. "Looks like you've had a good innings, eh?"

Manoeuvring the massive beast, Fred tugged at the makeshift bridle. The horse's legs stumbled as it turned. It gave a concerned snort, pulling its head in the opposite direction.

"Shush, fella. Easy now."

As the steed settled, Fred wrapped the reins around a sturdy hook on the back wall, sealing the final fate of the poor creature. Peering around the tarp, a curious David watched Fred pick up a big pair of shears. The horse whinnied softly as the mane was clipped so closely it was shorter than the stubble on a barber's old bristle brush. Fred put each handful of the hair in one of two hessian bags slung around his waist. Gould made a pretty penny selling this particular by-product to the local upholsterers for tassels, braids and stuffing. Next to go was another valuable resource with a myriad of uses—the tail—removed in one swift flick of the skilled knife man's blade. That would be resurrected as violin bows, artist's brushes, even fishing flies. Fred looped it up in a loose knot and popped it in the other bag.

The masterful workman moved forward and gently stroked the horse's cheek, still whispering in his calm and soothing voice. The stallion nuzzled its nose towards him, its misty grey breath showing up against the moonlit sky.

David saw the slaughterman grab an old apron covered in congealing blood. Quick as a flash, he enveloped the beast's head in it, blinding the thing instantly. It was a trick of the trade Fred had learned early on in his career. Reaching for his poleaxe, a firm thwack was applied to the animal's brow. Its suffering was over. With a tremendous bloodcurdling tremor, the body dropped dead onto a sheet covering the flagstones. Frozen to the spot in horror, young David's stomach turned at the ghastly sight.

"Don't just stand there, David. Give me a hand."

The heavy thud was a signal to drag the corpse to another dark corner of the yard. It housed a spacious 'kitchen', lined with six floor-level bubbling coppers, the steam rising against the whitewashed walls. Sickened, David took two good handfuls of the sheet as he and his cousin began to heave the corpse out of Fred's way. Convinced its soulless goggle-eyes were still looking at him, he closed his own and yanked with all his might. Heave! Heave!

"Oi! Watch your step, Davey!"

Noah's underling snapped his eyelids open and saw his feet teetering by the rim of one of the boilers. Panicked, he yelped in fear and jumped to safety. Together they manhandled the beast around and lashed its fetlocks around a sturdy wooden pole. Then, Noah gave a cast-iron winch a few clunking turns. The horse's body was now dangling a couple of feet in the air, its lifeless head trailing on the floor. David watched wide-eyed as Noah took a chisel and prised off the precious horseshoes, then flinched as he used a knife to hack off all four hooves.

"Johnny! Got one ready for you!" Noah boomed.

"Thanks, lad. On my way."

Stubbing out his cigarette, Johnny, the leather worker, sauntered over. He began stripping off the hide in large sheets. Once an area of skin was removed, Fred began to flay the flesh from the bones. Huge bloodied chunks were thrown into one of two wheelbarrows—the better-quality meat went into one barrow, the gristle and offal into another. David's eyes widened in disbelief. Noah explained more as his bloodied hands gathered up the bones and tossed them aside into yet another barrow.

"Those hooves there will become some posh fella's inkwell or salt cellar, Davy."

Although he continued with his induction, Noah wasn't sure his underling was listening. "East End cats are fussy things. They prefer meat. Dogs are far less picky and will happily sink a portion of tripe. Don't just stand there. Help me. If Gould sees you standing with your hands in your pockets, he won't be pleased."

David wheeled the stripped bones over to a monstrous mincing machine, where Noah gave him a demonstration of the next step. Deftly, the older lad navigated the barrow's front wheel along a narrow plank lying on top of a short flight of stairs. At the top step, Noah flung the handles up, and the whole load tumbled into the gaping mouth of a huge metal chute. He pressed a big button, and after some considerable grinding, the mangled mess slopped out of a tube and into a large wooden barrel.

"Bring me the next one, David!" yelled Fred, above the rumbling of the mincer.

Mustering all his resolve, the young lad untethered the next horse. David shuddered as the mare looked him in the eye and gave a soft whinny. I ain't looking round that curtain this time.

David hoped one day he could feel that at home in the knacker's yard.   For now, the marginally better rates of pay would be his compensation for enduring the horrors of the night shifts. Before he started at Gould's, Noah told him there were plenty of men who worked their way up the ranks, men who saved enough money to set up their own farm or stables in the country, free from the choking smog of the capital.

Back at the mincing machine, another lad paused it briefly, swapped in a fresh barrel, then fired the device up again. The foetid tub of slurry was wheeled off to the rendering area to be boiled down, and the fat removed. A boy, about ten, skimmed off the floating beige grease with a ladle and put it into pails to solidify.

Noah continued his commentary.

"The gaffer sells that gloop to saddlers for lubricating and protecting leather harnesses. When it comes to stopping the wheels of carriages squeaking, London cabbies swear by Gould's Proprietary Axle Grease. Candle makers are fond of it too."

Surprisingly, there was still something to be salvaged from the poor old horse's remains.

"The bones are dried, powdered, then sold for fertiliser."

Stretching by the main entrance were neat rows of sacks, full to the brim with the processed bonemeal. Alongside them was a crate of used horseshoes ready to be fitted to lucky new incumbents. Then, finally, there was a fully loaded wagon piled high with sacks of leather destined for the tanneries at the leather market on Weston Street.

"That leather might become a German cavalryman's trousers or the roof of a Brougham carriage. Not a single piece of those beasts is left unprocessed."

David was appalled and impressed in equal measure. Who knew so much useful stuff could come from a horse? Noah looked over at Fred and saw two full barrow loads of meat ready for boiling.

"Come on, let's wheel these over to the pans."

The lads took one barrow each towards the ominous copper cauldrons.

"One of these can take three good-sized horses. If they are big, like shires, the pot can still fit two. Just be thankful there were no rotting corpses today. They smell awful as they simmer. It's quicker with good nags. In an hour and twenty minutes, the meat will be ready—rotten flesh needs another hour to make it safe."

David closed his eyes and tipped his barrow of offal into the bubbling pit. He heard it slither down the gritty metal chute and land with a loud splosh. The rest of the horses were dispatched and dismembered as the first batch cooked. By now, the new boy was a nervous wreck. When asked, he blamed his trembling on the cold.

"Ciggie, Davey," Johnny the leatherman enquired.

"Please!"

Once it was ready, the two Sewell lads took the meat out with big wire ladles and laid it on some raised stones in a huge metal bath.

"Start pouring some buckets of cold water in. We need to get this ready for collection. The first of the meat hawkers will be here by six."

David's arms ached as the mountain of meat was moved. Fred carefully hacked the finished product into manageable chunks, ready for folks like Mabel's father to take it out with them on their rounds.

"There will be one price for the flesh and another price for the offal and tripe, Davey. Are you alright lad, you look a bit peaky?"

The poor chap swallowed hard, his tortured stomach now doing somersaults.

"All the lads at the yard know it is supposed to be destined for cats and dogs, but sometimes, it ends up in the belly of a poor beggar."

Davey rushed off and wretched in the corner. The old hands had a good chuckle at the new boy.

"You'll need to toughen up a bit, lad." joked Fred. "When you've finished chucking your guts up, you can help us get ready for the customers, boyo. They'll be here in an hour."

6

DOWNWARD SPIRAL

Joe and Ruth arrived at the yard a little later than usual at just gone six, delayed as they rowed about Billy. Ruth was adamant she should take care of the baby, and no amount of convincing from Joe would change her mind. Mabel hid under the blankets and waited for it to blow over. In the end, Joe relented. Precious time slipped away, forcing his hand, and, with reluctance, he caved in. The later he got to the knacker, the more likely he was to get the dregs. Saturday was his best day on his route around Clerkenwell, and he needed the prime cat meat, not the offal, to make a killing.

The weary couple's faces fell when they saw a long line of sellers snaking away from the main entrance. Joe grimaced. Ruth smoothed her hand over the shawl, feeling the reassuringly warm lump of her son swaddled beneath. She peered inside, and his little face beamed up at her. It seemed Lady Luck was with the Nithercotts that morning. Not only did Billy seem in fine fettle, but the lengthy queue ahead of them quickly evaporated too.

Back at the family home, Mabel was also pleased, noting the overnight rain had abated. She hoped the good weather would make her parents' day a little sweeter. Another night of acrimony was the last thing she wanted.

'Please let there be no arguing in this house tonight, Lord? Please?' she prayed, looking up and crossing both sets of fingers to ensure her plea was heard.

"Morning, young, Noah," Joe chirped as he flung open the lid of his bright barrow.

"I'll take twenty pounds worth today. I'm feeling positive! Today's Miss Wilmot Day, my dad!"

"A-ha! Right you are, Joe! Say no more," Noah chuckled. "Just give us a second."

He nodded for a green-looking David to measure out the order.

"That'll be ten shillings, please."

"Ten? Daylight robbery! No bulk discount?"

"No, Joe. Mr Gould will string me up like one of his old nags."

Sullen and belligerent, Joe counted out the money then thrust it at Noah.

"Here."

The wet flesh slid off David's weighing scales and thumped into Joe's barrow. Ruth looked on, sickened by the atmosphere in the slaughterhouse. She muttered that 'if his nibs reckons I'm coming here with him again, he's got another thing coming!'

Joe fished the money out of his trouser pocket, then headed off speedily to Granville Square where his best customer lived.

"Here, want to put that tray on the barrow for a bit?" Joe asked his wife, taking it off her before she could answer. "There you go. I bet that's easier, eh?"

Ruth's eyes narrowed with contempt. He was always overly nice after being grouchy and cruel. Joe's barrow rumbled over the cobbles in the direction of Clerkenwell as the morning sun peeped over the grey roofs. Looking like it could topple off at any moment, she grabbed the tray back.

"Don't. Just don't. Let's get today over with and get back home."

Joe had learned over time that the best routes for him were along streets lined with the houses of tradesmen, mechanics, and labourers. The coachmen in a tucked-away mews were also a good bet as they always had a hungry German shepherd on patrol.

As a rule, Joe tried to avoid the old maids. They loved to tug at his heartstrings asking for meat on credit for little Tiddles, but after one or two of them had not paid, he decided they were best avoided—except for

Miss Wilmot. She was different. She was his best and most loyal customer by far.

Joe marched ahead like a well-trained infantry man, leaving Ruth, burdened with Billy, trailing in his wake.

"Keep up, Ruthie. What were you saying about getting home early?" he teased.

On the way, Joe suddenly let the trundling barrow grind to a halt in a rough-looking area. The tenement doors were sack cloth curtains. A few ragged children watched them like hawks deciding if they were worth pickpocketing or not. Their bare feet were black, and their noses dribbly.

"Here, look after the barrow, will you?" he whispered before vanishing down a dark alleyway, taking her tray with him.

"Don't leave me alone, Joe," she hissed, but there was no reply.

She pushed the cart forward a couple of yards to get a better view, then peered into the gloom. Joe's footsteps faded away and were replaced by two sharp whistles. A man in the shadows came to meet Joe at his front door, then began placing some things on the tray. Her husband glided back, carrying several pieces of delicate glassware.

"What on earth is that?"

"I had a chat with Hook-Handed Alf in the Drummer Boy last night. His mate, Jack, wants these, err, off-loading. They'll make us more than the rock cakes. We get fifty per cent."

Alf's associate was Jack Stead, a notorious local fence.

"I don't want to know, Joe. It's dodgy, this."

Watching from their doorway, the couple of wily little street urchins planned their attack.

"Are you two up to no good again," hissed their mother's voice as they felt her hands drag them back in.

Ruth was dismayed at the stock: cut-glass salt cellars, ashtrays, blue glass dessert plates, vinegar bottles, none of which seemed worth much, certainly not worth the risk of having your collar felt for dealing in stolen goods. The ornate pieces would be easy to identify by the rightful owner or a bobby on the beat.

"Shift this little lot, and I can get my coat back. And we'll have enough for next week's rent. Maybe a night in the music hall?"

She shot daggers at her husband, but he was having none of it. For Joe, the matter was settled. Ruth was to sell Jack's bent gear, and that was that. He knew it would sell at a reasonable price out on the streets or round the corner at the market. People there loved any old rat, although they called it bric-a-brac.

"Stop giving me the evil eye. We need the money to cover yesterday's shenanigans and pay McGinty the rent next Friday. It is not my fault we're short this week, remember."

He thrust the tray into her hands and threw the rope handle over her head. Billy struggled in the swaddling clothes, but there wasn't time to stop; Joe needed to be the first meat man in the area. Sellers would often trek fifteen to twenty miles to milk a good patch. Leaning into the handle, he shoved the barrow along with Ruth, following a few paces behind. The fragile glassware slid and jangled. Joe turned to look at her.

"Careful, love, eh?"

Ruth glared.

As Joe's barrow creaked along the cobbles, Ruth trailed even further behind, battling with Billy and the precarious merchandise. Furious, she cursed under her breath. *'I bet he picked this bleedin' stuff up on purpose. At least me rock cakes bounce if I have a mishap. Dust 'em off, and they're good as new. He can bloody well explain to Hook-Handed Alf about any breakages.'*

But it wasn't all bad news for the Nithercott's, a rare stroke of luck was coming.

7

MISS WILMOT'S EXTRA MOUTH TO FEED

Twenty minutes later, they reached Miss Wilmot's Clerkenwell townhouse. A modern development, Granville Square was spacious and attractive, with the ground floor of each dwelling painted a warm shade of ivory, a vivid contrast from the usual grime-covered buildings in the surrounding area. The two red-brick storeys above were peppered with rows of matching cream window sills and frames.

"Leave this to me. See if you can shift some of Jack's stuff in the meantime."

Ruth huffed at the suggestion.

"It's so early. There's no one about to ply anything to, never mind this tat."

"You'll get nowhere with that attitude. You'd better buck your ideas up."

Joe skipped up the steps to the entrance. He straightened his neckerchief, smoothed his waistcoat, knocked loudly, then waited for the door to creak open.

"Ah, Mr Nithercott, It's good to see you! You never let me down," trilled the old spinster, hands clasped to her heart as if praying to the saviour himself.

"No, I don't, Miss Wilmot, proper professional me. Always a pleasure to serve your good self. Come now, choose what you want."

He raised his hand like a regency lord offering to escort Miss Wilmot down the three short steps to the pavement. She tottered along, clutching a big metal bucket. Ruth watched Joe, marvelling at how much he fussed over the woman—quite a change from his cold and callous behaviour at home yesterday evening when he said Billy would be better off dumped in the canal.

"How much can I do you for today? Got it lovely and fresh this morning, barely an hour ago. Prime stuff this," he advised, raising the lid with a flourish.

Transfixed, Miss Wilmot peered in, not flinching in the slightest.

"Look at that lovely stuff. A bit more than usual, I think, my good man. Ten pounds should do it."

"Right you are."

"I know I shouldn't have, but I picked up a couple more strays this week, and they both look like they need a good feed. How some people treat these cats, well, it riles me, Mr Nithercott. Awful."

Joe picked out a series of meaty chunks, bouncing each one in his hand carefully to reassure Ethel she was getting her money's worth, then dropping it in the bucket.

"And a bit extra for luck, eh?" he added with a cheeky wink. "That do ya?"

Ethel grinned.

"Tell you what—how about a special price today? You have ordered a bit more. Twenty shillings? That's two off since it's you."

"Oh, you are a good 'un, Mr Nithercott. Will you help bring it upstairs?"

"Your wish is my command, my lady!"

Ruth rolled her eyes at the mock show of chivalry as Joe bundled the old lady and the bucket inside and prepared to negotiate the stairs to the first floor. Ethel loved his visits and banter. He was like a whirlwind who swept in and breathed precious life into her lonely existence. Wincing, Ruth slammed the barrow closed, keen to escape the steaming stench of horse meat. She balanced her tray on the lid and checked on Billy. *'Bless him, he's sound asleep.'* She stroked the lad's cheek.

"That's right. You show your dad you can be
a good boy, then you can come out again."

Miss Wilmot kept her home clean and tidy. The tiled hallway floor was immaculate with its black and white chequered pattern. The tall skirting boards were pure glossy white, and the dark bannister smooth and polished. A delicate chandelier and plush striped wallpaper completed the decor.

Once upstairs, Ethel tried to slide the sash window open with a heave, then grimaced, barely budging it an inch.

"Ah, my hands are playing up today, Joe.
Wretched arthritis. Would you mind feeding
them?"

Joe grabbed a piece of meat out of the pail and launched it out of the window. It landed on a small shed roof that housed Miss Wilmot's old outdoor privy and the coal house.

Within seconds, most of Ethel's rescue cats galloped up the rough wooden walls then paced and prowled around the meat like lions round a freshly-killed gazelle. They sniffed and pawed at a few slivers formed by the force of the impact, then lapped them up. Next came the scrabbling as they chomped on the flesh like greedy pigs scoffing in a trough.

"Look at them, Mr Nithercott. They can't get enough!"

The squabbling was intense: biting, fighting, yelping, hissing, each one wanting to fill its belly first on that wintery morning.

"It's chaos down there, Joe. They really should have better table manners, show a bit of gratitude don't you think?" mused Ethel. "Be a poppet and out a couple more pieces, then stop. If we put it all out, the greedy little blighters will wolf the lot and expect more tomorrow."

Joe was amazed the cats didn't injure themselves in their furious scramble for food. He launched two more lumps of meat, trying hard not to hit one of Ethel's feline friends around the chops. Not good for business, that.

"They're loving this, aren't they, Miss Wilmot?"

There was no reply.

"Miss Wilmot?"

Concerned, he turned to see the spinster in her own little world clutching the tiniest of black kittens to her bosom, stroking its head as it purred with contentment.

"Who's this little fellow?"

"A new addition. I've called this one Hercules—he'll grow into the name," she joked.

"How many cats is that now, Miss Wilmot."

"More than ten. Twelve maybe? It varies. They come and go when they please, of course. I sometimes wonder if I own them or they own me. You can never help too many animals in need, Mr Nithercott. Besides, this one stole my heart. Only the best meat for this little chap."

Joe grinned. More money for him!

"Is that everything? Need anything else?"

Ethel shook her head as she nuzzled the kitten.

"I'll see you next week then?"

"Perhaps Wednesday? Mr Nithercott, they'll eat this lot in no time with this cold snap we're having."

"Right you are."

A thankful Joe trotted downstairs then counted his money, delighted he had already turned a healthy profit, and it was barely breakfast time. He bade her a cheerful farewell as the door swung closed. The day's takings jingled in his pocket as Joe skipped down the steps.

"Ready for the next stop, Ruth?"

His wife was trying to calm Billy. The yelling hadn't started, but he was fidgeting.

"Ruth! Next stop?"

"What? Oh, right, yes. I suppose so."

Keen to not get another ear-bashing, she stroked Billy's head under the shawl in an attempt to soothe him.

"It had better be near a market, or I'll never sell this stuff," she complained as she picked up the tray and did her best to balance it as she fought with the rope neck strap.

Just then, Ethel's door opened, and she looked directly at Ruth.

"Do forgive my manners, my dear. I was so keen to feed my cats I forgot to introduce myself. Are you Joe's wife, by any chance?"

Joe puffed his chest out with pride.

"She is! This is the girl who won my heart!"

Ruth flinched at the words. Why did he always have to put on that charade? If only this old dear knew the real Joe Nithercott.

"Show me what you've got on that tray of yours, will you, lass?"

"Just some old glassware, Ma'am. Nothing special."

"I'll be the judge of that, dearie. Can you come up here?"

Ruth tiptoed up the stairs then cringed as Joe barked:

"That's top-notch stuff there."

"You have got some nice things, haven't you, my sweet?" said the kindly spinster, perusing the woeful wares.

"I have?"

"Yes."

Ethel's wiry hand reached across and took one piece and inspected it in the light.

"This is a nice sturdy bowl. I'll take it. Looks perfect for Hercules."

"Hercules?"

Joe piped up:

"Miss Wilmot's new kitten."

"Oh, I see. How about—"

Ruth dug around in her head for a price for the item, not wanting to fleece the old woman but also desperate to make enough to cover the rent after Jack Stead took his half.

Mid-calculation, Billy began to wail in agony. Ruth forgot all about the transaction and peered at the lump under the shawl—so did Miss Wilmot.

"How old's this little chap, then? He's got a fine pair of lungs on him!" she said, leaning over.

When the old spinster saw the extent of his emaciation, she winced. She'd taken in many a stray feline in better fettle. A bag of bones, she saw the sunken cheeks below his dark hollow eye sockets.

"He's three months," said Ruth, looking down, stroking some dribble off the child's chin.

"What a bonnie lad he is. Three shillings should cover it."

"It?" Ruth asked.

"The bowl, dear. I'll give you three shillings. Seems a fair price to me for something of this quality."

The young woman was going to ask if Ethel was sure it   was worth that much, then thought better of it as the benevolent spinster handed over the coins. Despite Joe lumbering her with that old tat, heaven's above, she made a sale.

"Thank you!" Ruth trilled as the coins jingled into her palm. Delighted, she looked at her husband with a look that meant 'let's go--before she changes her mind! Maybe it will be the music hall for us this week!

Ruth gave a little curtsey as Joe waved Miss Wilmot farewell. Back at the barrow, her husband held his hand out.

"I'll take that, thank you," he demanded.

Every barrow boy in the area wanted a slice of the wealthy spinster's business, but Joe made sure that none of the other sellers got a look in. Anyone who tried to convince Ethel that they offered a better deal was threatened with a good walloping. He'd learned the cat-meat trade from his father. It used to be a reasonable living, but now it was getting more competitive, with more and more peddlers fighting over the finite amount of meat available. He had dreamed of becoming a slaughterer, like Fred Kemp, a far more lucrative profession. But, for Joe, a slaughterer's life wasn't to be. There was fierce competition for those positions at the knacker's yard, and a father tended to follow in his son's footsteps, making it a closed shop to ambitious outsiders. With a grunt and a heave, his barrow began to move once more, and the couple made their way to their next stop on Joe's round.

"Twenty-three glorious shillings, Ruthie. With all this money, we can get Billy proper help. Maybe get a wet nurse to look after him at home? It'll turn out alright, you'll see. If our luck continues like this, the rest of our stuff will go soon, and we can knock off early, eh?"

They meandered along, selling dribs and drabs of meat as they went. A few people took a polite interest in Ruth's stock, but she only sold one more piece that morning. The rope strap was biting into her neck, and she kept pulling at it to have a break from the chafing. Staying in one spot in the market with customers coming to her was preferable to walking around the streets three paces behind Joe. Trailing behind, simmering, she watched a grinning Joe tip his hat to all and sundry, hoping to sell the last morsels of meat.

Eventually, she called out:

"Can we slow down? Or head to the market. No one wants this, Joe. It's all useless odds and sods."

"Chin up, girl. I've managed to sell nearly all of mine. I'll finish that off walking back to the market. Then we'll shift your stuff."

"No one wants it!" she hissed. "Why couldn't you have let me sell my rock cakes? Fresh and hot, on a cold morning, they lived up to their name."

The light rain that had followed them on and off since they left Granville Square had worsened. Big raindrops danced on the pavement and rippled the muddy puddles that formed in the road.

Back at Prospect Street, Mabel looked at the grey sky and the drizzle. She was fuming as there would be no chance of drying the laundry fully today either. As she came up the alleyway, she glanced about for her parents—but there was no sign. Her father often came home early on a Saturday if things had gone well. She hoped they would be back soon, before the weather got any worse, for Billy's sake more than anything else. Joe smiled at his wife.

> "Come on. I'll get you a pie, Ruthie. It's been a good day, so we can afford tuppence for a couple of hot pies. Treat ourselves, eh? Then, we'll shift Jack's stuff and toddle off home early. How about that, princess?"

> "Go on then. I'm famished."

Exmouth Market was bustling with shoppers eager to spot a bargain. The heavenly smell of hot pastry wafting along the street guided them to the pie man.

> "Here, you get a seat on that low wall. I'll bring 'em over. Back in a jiffy."

Relieved, Ruth was able to set down her tray for the first time in ages. Her soft nape was now red raw.

> "Here you go," Joe mumbled through a mouthful of pastry.

The steaming pie warmed Ruth's chilled fingers. The hot meaty filling tingled her tongue as she savoured each bite. With her left hand, she stroked Billy's hand under her shawl. No response. She teased back the garment. The child felt ice cold. It appeared that the borrowed oilskin had done nothing to keep him warm and dry. Her knees buckled under the heavy weight of reality. Her thighs knocked the tray. As it landed on the market's muddy floor, the glassware shattered, shards skeeting everywhere. Spinning on his heels, Joe panicked. 'That careless woman!' he simmered. 'Jack Stead isn't going to be best pleased.'

Ruth, trying to awaken Billy, was shaking him as vigorously as she would plump up a pillow. Seeing her, Joe's anger abated, and his worry took over.

> "We need to take him to the hospital again!
> Look! He's not right! He's almost blue.
> There's something wrong. He's not respond-
> ing to anything."

Like the boy who cried wolf once too often, today, the onlookers did nothing. Seeing the lad falter again so soon meant they had less patience with the Nithercott's predicament today. People were less sympathetic, less generous, less helpful. The mood amongst the market traders was dark. To them, the Nithercotts were clearly selfish people, bringing their foolish problems on themselves.

> "Will none of you lot even watch my bar-
> row?" Joe seethed.

There was no response. The long walk to the charity hospital began. Joe wheeled the empty barrow in front of him like greased lightning as Ruth ran alongside, trying not to trip over her long skirt as they dodged through the crowds. Quickly becoming exhausted, they had to rely on grit and determination to keep going.

The double doors at the hospital reception smacked open as Joe's barrow careered into them. He strode over to the desk.

"It's my lad again. Please help!"

The feisty and efficient receptionist gave a loud sigh. 'Why don't these people ever listen?' she fumed as she looked for their notes in yesterday's pile of yet-to-be filed papers.

"Please take a seat, Mr Nithercott. You'll be dealt with in due course. As you can see, we are quite busy today."

With no seats left, Joe glared at the nearest, healthiest looking person until they weakened and gave up their place. He spun his trance-like wife around by the shoulders and pushed her down. Increasingly distraught, Ruth rocked back and forth, cooing at the sickly child. His eyes would flicker every now and then, but more like a twitch than a conscious movement. She put her hand on his chest, hoping some of her strength would flow into him, like a healer in the bible, raising the boy like Lazarus from his grave. Her endeavours appeared to be in vain.

A beleaguered junior doctor stepped into the waiting room, and his expression stiffened. Them again? He was tired of spending his time fighting a losing battle with the working classes. Earning an income always trumped preserving their health. Whilst understandable, the practice dragged down the hospital's performance figures. The mortality rate was shared at the monthly donor meetings and with London's Board of Health. Philanthropists, keen to raise the poor up, would quickly move to another charity project if they felt their money was not making a difference.

Joe noticed his barrow was blocking the aisle, and he dragged it to one side, almost running over the doctor's foot in the process. The physician gazed down in frustration.

"Doctor Pennington! Please help us! It's our Billy again."

He looked at the three bedraggled figures in front of him.

"I see you took your son out today? Against my express orders?"

He strode over to Ruth and pulled the shawl, and flinched. He decided that the desperate child was on the verge of death.

"I suppose you'd better come through, Mr Nithercott."

"Oi!" yelled a sinister voice.

A mountain of a man stood up, blocking the doctor's path. Nursing a heavily bandaged hand, blood seeped through the dressing and dripped on the floor.

"Feckin' queue jumpers. I've been waiting here for an hour, so I have. What about me?"

Undeterred, Joe manhandled the clunky street barrow towards the examination room, the corner of it bashing into the labourer's thigh. The man swung a punch at Joe but missed.

The angry doctor put his foot down.

"Leave that confounded thing where it is, Mr Nithercott! Miss Bradshaw, keep an eye on this cart! And will you please calm down, Sir?"

The irate physician wrenched Joe's hands off the handle, and the two scolded parents paced behind, praying he could save their boy.

"He will save him, won't he Joe," whispered Ruth.

"Course he will," said Joe, squeezing her shoulder affectionately, unable to look her in the eye as he delivered his little white lie.

8

DENIAL

"He had a really good night last night, doctor. We went straight home and rested him like you said. He got some shut-eye, and he ate some broth. I fed him my milk too. He seemed chipper this morning. We thought I could stay at home with him and look after him with a good day's sales behind us. We were trying to do what you told us, but Saturday is Joe's best day—"

Pennington humphed. Ruth made a small soft bed on the examination table with her shawl, then undid the sling and oilskin holding Billy in position.

"I know we did wrong now, Doctor. But our landlord doesn't like his folks getting in arrears. So, if we end up homeless or in the workhouse, it'll be the end of my little lad. I just know it."

Ruth began to cry as the doctor took his stethoscope from under his white coat and pressed it to the baby's bare chest.

"His sores have been improving. My daughter helps him with that. We just need to feed him up a bit more. Should we hold off fixing his feet for now? But, if he's crippled, surely that's worse?"

The physician looked gravely concerned, the child thoroughly unresponsive. He listened for breath, but there was none. Through the pale paper-thin skin at Billy's wrist, he felt no pulse. Pennington suspected the poor lad's heart had just given out, too weak to beat. Desperate for fuel, his body had been forced to eat itself to survive, and now the cupboard was bare. Malnutrition had finally taken him.

The doctor traced his fingers along the boy's scalp and felt the fuzzy hair had fallen away in clumps. The poor mite's ribs stuck out like ridges on an accordion. He looked like a little bag of bones because he was. He must have been losing weight since he was born. Pennington unravelled the bandages. No longer restrained, his deformed feet curled over one another awkwardly. Too poor for nappies, the swaddling cloth was heavily soiled.

"Is he unconscious, doctor? Do something!"

"I'm afraid it's too late. He's gone."

Ruth collapsed into Joe's arms. Secretly, the doctor was relieved the frail tot had finally slipped away, the mother's obstinacy hastening the inevitable.

"Let me get him cleaned up a little bit," said Pennington.

Leaving the bereft parents in the cold whitewashed examination room, he enveloped Billy in the shawl and disappeared through the double doors. Joe squeezed Ruth's hand so tightly her knuckles cracked.

"Probably going to take him to the mortuary. They're good at cleaning people up. Then we can take him home."

Ruth nodded tearfully. Silent and reflective, they watched the second hand of the wall clock tick round and round. The doctor was gone for quite some time, and the longer he was missing, the more fretful the boy's parents became. Worse, the crowd in the waiting room were on the warpath, shouting at the poor receptionist, demanding to know why no one had been called for what felt like an age.

Alas, Pennington hadn't gone to clean Billy up. Instead, he'd gone to a basement office, the coroner's office, deep in the bowels of the hospital.

"I think you need to see this, Hubert", said the young medic as he unfurled the shawl. "A clear case of wilful neglect. Look how scrawny the lad is. I told them he needed bedrest and food, but well, as you can see, tragically, that advice—"

"—fell on deaf ears as usual?" the coroner mused as he examined the little body.

"How are we supposed to convince the donors we are doing a good job when our advice is ignored again and again? I think you need to take it further. Make an example of this sorry case. These East End types need to learn that they can't keep having children and failing to feed them. The soup kitchens should provide a safety net for those in basic need, not cutting-edge hospitals. And with the out-relief from the parish union, there is no reason for a child to starve to death in this day and age. It's scandalous. If we keep bailing them out, the poor are never going to change. We can't save them all. They have to save themselves—with the help available."

"I agree. Leave it with me."

He removed the child from the shawl.

"I'll start the autopsy now. Give this back to the mother," said the coroner, folding up the damp cloth.

"Oh, and before you do that, see if you can see PC Halsey on his beat. Ask him to arrest them and put them in the cells. This is a police matter. I am convinced of it. But there are certain formalities to navigate beforehand. I'll summon a coroner's hearing first thing tomorrow. That will clear a path for the police to gather evidence for a public prosecution."

The examination room swung open. Pennington appeared with the empty shawl. The distraught mother screeched:

"Where's my Billy? Where's my boy? I want to take him home!"

Joe's mouth fell open as he saw PC Halsey and two other officers in support following behind. Halsey was even bigger than the angry labourer. Joe gave up any hopes of making a run for it.

"Joe and Ruth Nithercott. I'm arresting you under suspicion of wilful neglect. There is to be an inquest. You are to appear in the coroner's court on Monday to explain yourselves."

Moments later, Joe and Ruth were frogmarched to an awaiting Black Maria.

"Leman Street," said Halsey.

The name rang a bell for Ruth, and so it should. Leman Street was Abberline's manor, the chief inspector who had successfully failed to find the Ripper. Thrown into the dank cells, they were both left to reflect alone.

How did it come to this?

9

ABANDONMENT

At Prospect Street, there was a knock at the Nither-cott's door.

"Lydia! That was good timing." Mabel chirped. "Come on in. The kettle's going on. Fancy a cuppa? I've just finished my mother's long list of jobs."

The old woman said nothing.

"Please tell me you didn't hear them rowing this morning? Hammer and tongues it was. Did they wake you? If they did, sorry about that."

Mrs Kirkham took a seat at the tiny dining table, then pulled out the chair next to her.

"You'd better sit down, dear. I just heard something in McGinty's corner shop. It's about your ma and pa and little Billy   "

Lydia's news was too much for Mabel to take in. Mrs Kirkham left her sat in a daze, staring into space.

"I'll check on you tomorrow, and I'll come with you to the hearing."

*

Before she knew it, Mabel found herself in the gallery at the coroner's court, with Lydia in tow. The coroner spoke first.

"It is my considered opinion that the child's heart finally gave out, after weeks of his frail little frame eating itself to survive, eventually resorting to his own cardiac tissue. It was impossible to feed the boy properly on the cold streets. Furthermore, he struggled and became agitated because of their aggressive home treatment of his clubfoot. This also affected his propensity to feed. Dr Pennington, a junior physician at the charity hospital, warned the child needed urgent bed rest and food. However, his advice was ignored. On the very next outing, the child died."

A hush fell on the room apart from the tap, tap, tap of the stenographer's fingers, noting the coroner's crushing words. The two parents felt the gallery's chastising gaze boring into them.

"Therefore, this death was not one of natural causes but starvation through wilful neglect."

There was a unified gasp at the judgement. Ruth's knees buckled, and she sobbed into her elbow as she slumped over the lip of the dock. Joe took to his feet, standing tall and defiant. Two court ushers were needed to bundle him away and down to the cells. The coroner instructed the police to gather evidence to conduct a criminal conviction, and it didn't take them very long. Loose tongues at Exmouth market and the Little Drummer Boy soon gave them all the evidence they needed to secure a conviction. Just two days later, Joe and Ruth found themselves at Stepney Crown Court.

Deliberately designed to be confrontational, the lay-out of the dark courtroom was oppressive. On a raised platform at the back, the judge sat in an ornate wooden chair under a decorative carved canopy. His grey hair blended well with his wig. His flowing robes were as red as a grenadier guardsman's tunic. Glistening gold lettering on the chair's black leather backrest read: 'VR'. Lower down, in front of the judge, was the clerk's desk. Smartly dressed in a dark frock coat and grey trousers, the man perused some papers before his voice boomed out.

"The court calls Mr and Mrs Joe Nithercott."

Up to his left was the large box for the defendants. The court architects preferred to put the defendants on show so their every movement could be scruti-nised as the evidence was presented. The heads of the two ushers appeared, followed by the handcuffed defendants shuffling behind them. The officials guided the accused to their seats. At one corner sat Ruth, rubbing her hands together feverishly, her eyes darting around the room trying to make sense of the scene. At the other corner of the dock was her husband. Gazing straight ahead, motionless, in an attempt to seem stoic, Joe's emotions were betrayed by his Adam's apple dancing up and down in his scrawny neck with each anxious swallow.

To the right was an empty witness box, and beside that, two rows of solemn jurors.

The public gallery was taken up with some councillors, a handful of religious figures and a swathe of journalists, notepads flipped open, sharpened pencils at the ready, poised to scribble down every bit of salacious detail about the case. Jimmy McGinty's nephew, Jack, took his place at the far end of the row. Mabel sat with Mrs Kirkham, who gripped the young woman's hand like a vice. Mabel grizzled into her friend's ear:

"What's he doing here?"

The little rogue gave Mabel a sinister smile.

After Joe and Ruth pleaded not guilty, the prosecution addressed the court, painting a picture of callous parental neglect, declaring the Nithercotts to be a contemptible pair wanting to hasten their deformed child's demise, to be free of 'the burden'.

"My lord, it has been less than four weeks since another child, their daughter Esther Nithercott, died in their care."

The court was aghast. Joe snorted like an angry bull.

"The defendants preferred to put their own needs above those of their offspring—and that is why, at barely three months old, William Nithercott is now dead."

The furious father felt every muscle tense like iron, his hands curled tighter than a fairground boxer preparing to deliver a sucker punch. Rocking in her seat, crumbling mentally, Ruth rubbed the tears from her cheeks then hid her face in her hands.

The most damning evidence from the witness box came from the coroner, Hubert Mitchell.

"Stepney Parish offers out-relief to the deserving poor who seek to keep in employment rather than enter to the workhouse. The mission and soup kitchen also offers assistance to families in need. Despite Dr Pennington's strict recommendation, the Nithercott's took the youngster with them on their costermonger route. The couple have a seventeen-year-old daughter, the twin of the deceased girl, acting as an unpaid domestic servant. The boy could, and should, have been left in Miss Nithercott's care."

The prosecutor turned to face the defendants.

"Despite this, you chose not to acccpt any outside assistance nor call on your daughter. Instead, you put your infant in danger knowingly and on purpose when you had access to safer options. The only consolation in this sorry situation is that your last surviving daughter is approaching adulthood and is now able to fend for herself."

The judge nodded. Scratching pens took verbatim notes of the scathing attack. Joe seethed. The coroner was addressed again.

"Mr Mitchell, I believe you have photographic evidence of the condition of the child upon death."

"Yes, Sir."

The prosecution's assistant passed copies to the judge and jury members who studied the images at length. Ever since the public fascination with the use of police photography to record the Ripper's ghastly activities, photographic evidence was captivating courtrooms and newspaper editors alike. The journalists craned their necks to see the pictures.

"The dark patches visible on the legs are the open sores, your honour."

The judge and jury winced as they looked at the images of his hideous clubbed feet, the shocking skeletal features, the emaciated frame. Unable to explain his side of the story, Joe's jaw locked tighter still. If Ruth hadn't disobeyed me that day, if I hadn't been in a rush to get the knackers yard, I wouldn't be in this mess. It's all her fault.

Too distraught to think, Ruth crumbled further into hopeless despair, her whole body trembling.

Several witnesses from Exmouth Market were called. All of them testified the sickly child should have been at home.

Unable to afford representation, Joe, and Ruth's attempts to put their side of the story across failed miserably. As an experienced orator, the prosecution soon tied them up in knots, driving gaping holes in their version of events. Mabel's own heart threatened to stop as her poor mother protested her innocence.

"I lost my Esther because I failed to watch over her. I was on an errand for my husband when the good Lord took her. For seventeen years, I cared for her with all my body and soul. There was never a shred of neglect."

She pointed up to the gallery, and all heads turned.

"My daughter, up there, she is the picture of health. I am not a bad person. Joe would have lost his cat meat route if he went into the workhouse or was forced to do out-relief work. Soon, we'd fall behind on the rent. We had no option but to carry on as we were. The charity hospital should have admitted him, helped us with his legs, not turned its back on us."

Several jurors nodded at the suggestion, looking upon Ruth with compassion. The others felt that her deliberate disobedience deserved harsh punishment.

After Lord Justice Scruton's summing up, it only took an hour for the jury to reach a decision.

"Would the foreman please rise?" he asked.

"On the charge of wilful neglect, what is your verdict for Mr Joe Nithercott."

"Guilty, my lord."

And Mrs Nithercott. Guilty or not Guilty?"

"Guilty."

Mabel froze, her entire life turned upside down by the short exchange.

"Members of the jury, you have found the Nithercotts guilty. I now turn to sentencing. The conviction of death by wilful neglect shall be liable at the court's discretion to a fine, not exceeding one hundred pounds or alternatively to imprisonment with or without hard labour, for any term, not exceeding two years."

Both Ruth and Joe gulped. They certainly couldn't afford such a steep fine, and the thought of up to two years of hard labour crucified them.

"Given your mental state, Mrs Nithercott, you will be sentenced to six months in Her Majesty's Prison Holloway."

At the mention of the dreaded place, Joe lost his temper and took one last futile attempt to protest their innocence, wrestling with the court ushers as they tried to restrain him.

"Mr Nithercott, I will not tolerate such outbursts. I find you in contempt of court. In view of the fact, you did nothing to control your wife and failed to insist she keep the child at home, you will be sentenced to two years of hard labour in Newgate prison."

The journalists flipped over their notebooks to start a new page of shorthand, scribbling ferociously. Ruth wailed as Joe was forcibly dragged down the stairs, still shouting and flailing. Mrs Kirkham swallowed hard. For seven hundred years, Newgate had a terrible reputation as London's darkest hellhole, and the prospect of the girl's father being imprisoned there was terrifying, especially now he would be demonised, labelled a 'child killer'. The young woman squeezed Lydia's hand even tighter as she watched her father being dragged away. She tried to make eye contact with her mother, but Ruth was led away like a lifeless draper's mannequin.

Slowly, the gallery and the jurors made their way out of the courtroom. Mabel was rooted to the spot, not ready to face being uprooted from everything she knew back on Prospect Street. Without her parents' income to provide for her, she knew she would end up in the workhouse—unless she could devise a last-minute, cunning plan. That would be tricky. All their neighbours barely made ends meet. Having another mouth to feed was not feasible. Secretly, she hoped Lydia would offer her a floor for a few days on the quiet while she got some pennies together. If she made more boxes for Jimmy, maybe she'd have a chance? Even if it was just a rope bed at some common lodgings. Anything but the workhouse! Her plotting was finally interrupted when she heard her name called.

"Mabel! Mabel, come on, poppet," soothed Mrs Kirkham. "Let's get you back, eh?"

Outside, as the stormy weather whipped around them, the two women hunched into the wind, walking in silence. The lack of an immediate offer of a bed from Lydia worried Mabel. She racked her brains for somebody else who would let her move in. Unfortunately, the shame of being the daughter of a couple of imprisoned parents would mean Mabel's options were limited.

Circumstances were holding the girl's feet to the flame, and it was time to act, if she was to avoid being badly burnt.

10

UNPALATABLE OPTIONS

"Here, drink this," said Lydia, thrusting a hot mug of tea into the lass's hand.

The poor girl's heart was breaking at the thought of no family members to rely on and not a single asset to her name.

"And, before you ask, my pet, the answer is no."

"Ask what?"

"To stay here with Harry and me. If Jimmy McGinty finds out you're staying here for free rather than paying for a bed at his lodging house, he'll string me up on a gibbet outside his corner shop. Harry can only just afford our rent as it is."

Mabel's eyes began to sting. She blinked hard, peered at the dark mug, staring as she swirled the brown liquid. Lydia looked across to the Little Drummer Boy, packed to the rafters with an army of bawdy folk intent on drinking their problems away. The contrast in atmosphere was pronounced.

"Talking of McGinty, Barry and that son of his have just let themselves in next door to your place. Be quick because, by the looks of it, they've got a handcart ready to strip it bare. You'd better get what's rightfully yours!"

Mabel's hands thudded against the door of number six, swinging it directly into Barry McGinty's back.

"Oi! Steady on! We're only collecting what's due, darlin'."

"I beg your pardon?"

"Well, Jimmy is due a week's rent. So, he'll have to sell what he can to cover your debts. Seems you might be lucky after all, though. Another family is moving in tonight, so he might settle for a bit less."

Barry glanced at his smirking son.

"Right, Jack. The furniture is Jimmy's, so that's staying, but all the small stuff like the plates and mugs—take all that. I'm sure Micky Pavlovich will be interested in 'em."

The lad put his arm on the top of the table and swept all the enamelware into a large hessian sack. Next went a small embroidered picture Esther had made. The sentimental value far outweighed anything the pawnbroker would give for it. Mabel charged towards Jack, tackling him like a scrum-half.

Jack circled his arm and wrestled free, almost hitting Mabel in the jaw with his elbow. Barry McGinty looked on and laughed.

"The whole family should have been locked up! Bunch of vagabonds."

Mabel broke free and dashed upstairs to retrieve a few mementoes from her childhood home. She took a small pillow case, hid her mother's comb and Billy's old comfort blanket within it, and then stashed everything under her apron. Finally, she flew downstairs past Jimmy's brutal henchmen and back to the safety of Mrs Kirkham at number four.

"I see they're not wasting time," Lydia lamented as a sack of the Nithercott's meagre goods and chattels landed on the cart. The girl shook her head, unable to speak.

"Well, it's time for you to look after yourself, my dear."

Mabel bit the inside of her cheek, trying to tame her tears and gripped the few trinkets she had liberated tighter still. Mrs Kirkham took her firmly by the shoulders and looked her directly in the eye, her head inches from the girl's face.

"Now, you listen to me, Mabel Nithercott. You're a good person. Don't let this sorry matter set you back. Do your best, and everything will fall into place. The Lord will take care of you. There is a sharp distinction between the deserving and undeserving poor. Remember that. It was something your father always talked about. And you're one of the most dedicated, loyal, and deserving people I've ever met."

The hot char was almost gone. Mabel's fingers trembled as she raised the mug to her lips, not wanting her final moment of safety to end. Once the drink was gone, she would be following soon after. She didn't want to tarry and miss the workhouse curfew. Suddenly, the girl gagged, then spat a mouthful of tea leaves back into the cup.

> "I know it doesn't feel like it now with all this looming over you, but in my bones, I sense some good will come of this. As if it will be the making of you? A fresh start? It'll only be a few months, and I'll be able to visit on Sundays—"

Lydia fell silent as some heavy boots crunched on the gritty flagstones by the porch. Thankfully, it wasn't one of McGinty's heavies, but her youngest son, Harry, returning home, tall, dark, and brooding. This time, he didn't greet Mabel with his trademark 'cheeky-chap' wink, thinking it inappropriate. The girl felt the spark between them rekindle. How she longed for him to take care of her, cosset and protect her. Harry had felt the spark too—but he got a tingle in his loins anytime a pretty girl crossed his path. He attempted a benevolent look. It worked. Her heart soared.

"I've just heard the news, Mabel. I wish there was something more I could do to help," he said, bowing his head. "In time, there will be, I am sure, but alas, not today. You're going to have to brave the workhouse, just until ma and I can figure out a plan for you."

"Thank you very much for helping. Both of you. You're all I have until my parents are released."

"I'll see if I can get you a job at the telephone exchange. My firm is installing all the cabinetry in the building."

"Really, Harry! You promise?"

"Promise. There is plenty of telephonist work now they are expanding the new network into Wales. Good job with excellent pay, by all accounts. Far better than a pretty face like yours getting mangled with phossy jaw with Bryant and May in Bow, eh?"

"That sounds wonderful! I will be eternally grateful."

Harry did his best to hide a lustful smirk. Mabel's empty mug landed in the middle of the dining table. Lydia glanced at the tea leaves nestled in the bottom and smiled.

"Want to know your fortune, my dear? It beggar's belief, but it's looking like a rosy one—"

"—No, thanks, Lydia." she said hastily, not wanting to prolong the painful farewell. "I'd better not be late."

She picked up the grubby white pillowcase and pulled her shawl around her once more. Out on the street, although it was only just past five, the sky looked dark and ominous. She kept her head low as she vanished into the inky blackness of the East End, not wanting to see her neighbours whispering about her behind their hands: 'Look! Mabel Nithercott, the child of the child killers'.

Sadly, her efforts were thwarted. Outside the Little Drummer Boy, a crowd of drunken women jeered her name and jabbed their fingers at her.

"Oi, Nithercott!" yelled a man's voice. "You owe me some money!"

Mabel's eyes took a gander about, looking for the source. Hook-Handed Alf! What could he mean? She didn't owe him a penny! She hunched over and melted into the crowd as Alf barged his way through the busy bodies. He scanned the street like a lion looking for the weak gazelle of the herd. Mabel decided not to risk taking a detour to drop off the comb at the pawn brokers

As well as avoiding Alf, Mabel needed to get to St Olave's workhouse, over two miles away, well before the six o'clock curfew bell rang. Given the arctic conditions that night, there would almost certainly be a long line outside the entrance.

Even if Mabel did have a few pennies, the common lodging houses were already teeming with the homeless. The attempts to free London from the grip of the slums, demolishing the tenements before new housing was put up in its place, meant that more and more people were crammed into one building. The situation worsened as Russians, Poles, and Jews, fleeing persecution on the continent, flooded Whitechapel to find lodgings near the bustling warehouses and docks.

Jimmy McGinty had mastered the art of concealing his own brand new slums in plain sight. He revelled in the laxer regulations applied to overnight stays in preference to the draconian building inspections that came with monthly rents. At number twelve alone, there were up to seventy people from across the continent regularly sleeping in coffin or rope beds. Jimmy planned to convert all his properties on the street to lodging houses. Tenement rooms meant he could only fleece a dozen families at one time. Seventy payees per night seemed a much healthier figure.

Mabel scurried to St Olave's to beg for mercy. She decided resorting to knee-tremblers behind the Little Drummer Boy with the likes of that brute Alf, just to pay for a coffin bed, seemed far worse.

Like a salmon swimming upstream, she dashing through the busy streets, packed with workers starting a shift or finishing one, she hoped she made it in time. If she didn't who knows where she might end up.

11

MEETING THE CURFEW

Young Mabel Nithercott walked up to the imposing entrance of the union workhouse. Recently opened, it was one of the most modern facilities provided by the Board of Guardians, but it still looked cold and menacing. No one in authority ever wanted the workhouse to look 'inviting'.

The gate warden was the first odious official Mabel encountered, a brusque and mechanical man with no patience for the local feckless and workshy. He had met too many of that sort in his time. Some earned a little more respect from him: those tramping from workhouse to workhouse, travelling long distances to take up agricultural or navvy work. At least they had a good reason to turn to the union, unlike this motley crew.

His critical eye scanned the ragtag bunch of people lined up before him. Imbecile. Always argumentative. Cripple. Drunk. Plastered. Hmm, who's this? There was something about Mabel that made the warden think she was one of the better ones. Maybe that was because the two women behind were staggering, jabbering, laughing, and joking behind her, smelling like a brewery from quite a distance away. In contrast, she seemed polite and reserved.

"We shouldn't have had that last gin, Ada. Should have spent the money on a bed at the mission. Better than this hell hole."

The warden agreed in silence. Why people turned up when they could easily get a rope bed for a penny at a common lodging-house perplexed him. Canny members of the underclass had the skills to pull a shady stunt on a hapless out-of-towner at one of the capital's many stations, drink away almost all their ill-gotten gains, come back late to the lodging house, tell tall tales to their fellow bounders, and leave with a thick head in the morning. There would be no such freedom and frivolity in the workhouse.

Mabel took another step towards the heavy doors, biting her lip. At least, there is no further to fall. This, hopefully, would be as bad as life got. Remembering Harry had promised to get her some work at the flourishing telephone exchange, she felt her stay was bound to be a short one. She just knew it. Her lip loosened out a little from the grip of her clenched teeth.

After giving her name to the warden, she walked into a small courtyard to the left to wait with the other folk in tonight's intake. A young family huddled together for warmth.

"What will happen to us, Pa?" said the elder child. "Papa? I asked you a question!"

The dark and brooding dull red building had two wings visible from the front, each with five floors. Behind it sprawled a massive segregated indoor and outdoor complex capable of housing over a thousand inmates. The creamy white entrance matched a myriad of painted window sills above.

Nobody spoke. When the six o'clock bell rang, two inmates hauled the massive doors shut. Two officials appeared from within who, moments previously, had also been watching the fresh faces arrive on the lookout for troublemakers. Mabel correctly guessed they were the master and mistress. Probably a married couple too, she thought.

The master swung a black cane in one hand, slapping it menacingly into his outstretched palm, like a gang member with a bat awaiting his nemesis. His tight-lipped expression ran away from his face. His jowls sagged as he stared at the battered bunch in front of him. In his top hat and long black coat, he towered over them. The scowling, pinch-mouthed mistress clasped her hands on top of her fat round belly.

"Is anyone afflicted with a disease?" he growled.

All the heads shook 'no'.

The master stopped tapping his cane and motioned towards the door with it.

"Go through there and wait for me at the other side."

The small gaggle of people looked at each other, waiting for someone to make the first move.

"Now!" he bellowed, making them jump out of their skins then scrabble for the door this way and that, like a herd of panicked sheep.

In the reception area, there was a large table. Above it was a sign:

"Let us not grow weary of doing good for in due season, we will reap if we do not give up."

It seemed the guardian's commitment to reform moral character began as soon as inmates arrived.

The master and mistress swept past the group and stood behind the admission desk.

"This workhouse prides itself on order, cleanliness and discipline. When you are under this roof, you will live by my rules. Is that understood?"

"Yes."

"Yes, sir, if you please? Separate yourselves into two groups. Men on the left, women on the right. And be quick about it."

A few of the older children were unsure where to stand. The mistress dealt with the matter swiftly.

"Any child aged seven or under may stay with its mother. The others will be separated from their parents and placed in male or female adult dormitories. You are not permitted to share a dormitory with a relative. Have I made myself clear?"

"Yes, Miss," answered a few meek voices.

Some of the younger children began to snivel at the news of their imminent separation. Mabel's gaze was drawn to a large poster on the wall. It listed the number of workhouse rules and regulations that had to be always followed to the letter and the penalties for breaking them.

Neglect of work: Dinner withheld.

Swearing: Solitary confinement for 24 hours on bread and water.

Damaging workhouse property: Two months (minimum) imprisonment.

One of the drunk girls, Peggy Prescott, began to hiccup uncontrollably, swallowing hard and holding her breath to stifle the spasms. The master glared at her.

"Sorry, Sir."

Hic.

"You will only speak when you are spoken to." he snarled. "Get into two rows."

The small groups did as they were told.

"You will now be washed, inspected for lice, then clothed in your uniform."

There were a few acknowledging grunts.

"Men, you will follow me. You women, follow the mistress. And be quick about it."

The two groups trooped in opposite directions down a narrow corridor and across their respective exercise yards into their wings. A few inmates were cleaning up after a long day's work. The master liked to make it clear to newcomers that this was a *'work'* house. His catchphrase was, "Do not let your hands be weak, for your work shall be rewarded." Exhausted washerwomen with large wicker baskets filled to the brim made their final trip to the linen storeroom. Across in what they assumed was the men's courtyard, they heard a regular thud as the male inmates tried not to blind themselves, smashing stones to smithereens with heavy lump hammers. By the entrance to the female quarters, the mistress stopped abruptly.

"In here, now."

The group obeyed without grumbling this time. Every minute they spent on the premises seemed to sap their souls a little more, making them more compliant. It wouldn't be long before they morphed into grey, shadowy versions of themselves, like the washerwomen they had encountered earlier. The stench of disinfectant was nauseating. Mabel noticed a wall rack with rough grey uniforms dangling from it. They appeared to be all the same size. Some were visibly worn. A large tin bath sat on the floor in the centre of the room, in full view of everyone—and anyone—in the vicinity.

"You will clean yourself thoroughly. Then, there will be the inspection. Decide amongst yourselves who will bathe first."

"Yes, miss."

Even though the group would have to reuse the same bathwater, no one wanted to go first. Irritated, the mistress gave them another stark warning then left them to it, busying herself with her duties elsewhere.

"Feel this uniform, Peggy! I've laid on better sacks down the docks—" joked Ada Fairfax.

"—they say all the nice girls love a sailor," Peggy replied with a giggle.

Each woman held a series of uniforms against themselves, trying to find one that fitted them, at least vaguely. It proved futile. Everyone found they were too baggy in some places and too tight in others. It was clear the garb was not meant to be comfortable. The door swung open again as the mistress stared at the bathtub. The lack of suds in it disappointed her.

"So, you have chosen to disobey me?" she growled.

With a bellyful of booze, Peggy Prescott went first, stripping off completely even though any Tom, Dick or Harry in the courtyard could see her, then plunged into the icy cold water.

The workhouse Mistress reached for the carbolic soap and threw it at her. She fumbled, and it landed with a splosh.

"Give yourself a good clean with the loofah. You're filthy."

"This is really toasssty, girls. Nothing to worry about," slurred Peggy, her hands searching under the water for the slippery bar. "It's bliss!"

"Enough of your insolence. Silence."

For the next person, the water would not be heavenly. Peggy hadn't washed for at least two weeks. The milky grey film left behind each bather thickened as the process rumbled on.

"Next one," screeched the cruel mistress.
"You, there. Yes, you. Come on," she yelled,
pointing at Mabel, then at the bath.

"Get in!"

Mabel did her best not to look at the foul water before getting in. As she pulled her skirt off, the pillowcase inverted, spilling its contents on the floor. The eagle-eyed mistress was furious.

"What is that?"

"Just a comb and a blanket from home. No contraband, miss."

"I'll be the judge of that."

"And this?" said the mistress, holding up a third item.

In her haste to leave, Mabel had also scooped up a small screw-top tin of Billy's balm within his blanket.

"Just some ointment. I must have picked it up by mistake—"

"—or tried to conceal smuggling something else in against the house rules."

Mabel tried and failed to remember the penalty from the long list on the admission room poster. The mistress snatched her belongings from her.

"These will be confiscated until you leave."

It was the last time Mabel would see her personal possessions for months.

"I suggest you women distance yourself from this woman. She is a bad influence. I can assure you, your time here will be much better if you obey the rules."

Mabel stripped off, feeling all eyes upon her as she stood there naked.

"Now bathe!"

The mistress gave Mabel a shove. Losing her footing, the poor girl toppled into the tub. Peggy and Ada guffawed at the spectacle. She felt like a performing circus animal, the centre of other people's merriment, yet experiencing no joy of her own.

"Scrub yourself harder."

The mistress watched Mabel rub her skin with the loofah until it was flushed with blood.

"Better."

The women who had already bathed stood around, staring at each other, adjusting their scratchy uniforms. In silence, they awaited the mistress's next instruction. The noise of the locks and metal doors that echoed around the building chilled their souls. Every ounce of freedom, every shred of individuality was systematically stripped from them, and there was nothing that they could do about it.

"All washed?"

Yes, Miss"

"In a line now. Face the wall."

The mistress inspected each woman, pushing any stray tresses of hair into a loose elasticated cap, checking the napes of their necks for any tell-tale bites.

"Turn around."

One by one, each woman's hands and fingernails were inspected. Finally, the mistress stopped at Ada, who didn't meet the required standard.

"Why can I see this dirt under your nails? You are a disgrace. It's people like you that bring disease into this place," said the mistress as she scrubbed the girl's hands.

"Mr McLaughlin, please take this woman to solitary confinement."

After a bit of a scuffle, Ada was escorted from the room. The mistress took Mabel by the shoulders as she turned her round to complete the inspection.

"Not bad."

"Everyone has folded their clothes ready for storage, Mr McLaughlin?"

"Yes, ma'am. We are ready for the footwear to be allocated."

Mr McLaughlin called two worker inmates into the room, both grappling with a box full of scuffed leather clogs. As she fought to get the clunky shoes on, Mabel could feel the stiff heel rubbing against the soft skin of her Achilles. She was in no doubt that the clogs were going to rub her ankle raw. All the women tried swapping between different pairs, but, once again, none seemed to fit. Matron was losing the last of her patience.

"We've wasted enough time. There is still much to do before the evening meal. Put your clothes in a storage box. Give Mr McLaughlin your name. Your belongings will be labelled and stored until your release."

Each woman proudly folded her 'civilian' clothes and laid the shoes on top.

"Quickly now. Follow me," screeched the mistress as she flounced along the corridor, still barking orders. "Do as you're told. May I remind you, there are no rewards, only punishments."

The women moved in double-quick time. Mabel felt her spirits sink lower. She'd never known what it was like to be powerful, but the little bit of choice she used to have in life ceased to exist. Now, she was utterly powerless. As the mistress led the new inmates to their dormitory, the clog-clad women followed close behind.

Although the dormitories were small, ten women were supposed to sleep in each one. The gloomy room was illuminated by a single gas light. In terms of fixtures and fittings, it was completely bare apart from a collection of iron beds and some shared chamber pots. The tiny windows were six feet off the ground and offered no views of the outside world. Several yards of blue and white striped fabric, as well as a large pile of loose straw, occupied the central floor space.

"You are lucky. You will be making your own fresh mattresses for tonight. Please take two pieces of fabric and begin stitching. I will return within the hour. Those who fail to finish in time will be forced to sleep on the floor."

Mabel collected her materials and made a start. Working by gaslight, the first challenge was threading the coarse cotton through the eye of the needle. She was fortunate to have younger eyes. An elderly woman in their group struggled to start until Mabel stepped in to help.

"I wonder how Ada is getting on? What do you reckon?" Mabel pondered to Peggy. "Solitary confinement sounds awful. How long will she be there?"

"Solitary, you say," piped up old Gertrude. "Been there myself once or twice. Got a bit lippy."

"And?"

"Truly a place to be feared, down in the basement. She'll be kept in complete darkness, with just a rickety old wooden cart to lie on. They used to be able to send little kids down there, but not anymore. The inspectors don't like it. Only adults these days. I hope she's not superstitious."

"Why?" asked Peggy.

"Well, it's next to the 'dead room,'" cackled Gertrude. "Still, with a few ghosts down there, she won't be on her own, eh?"

Mabel and Peggy stared, open-mouthed. Every time footsteps paced along the corridor, they expected a disappointed mistress, or a troubled phantom, to appear. The wait was tortuous. The women beavered away, working along all four sides of the mattress cover, only leaving a small gap at one end to admit the stuffing. There didn't seem to be enough straw for everyone to make theirs thick enough. The thought of being there until Harry got her a job brought out Mabel's selfish gene. She had to fight her conscience not to take more than her fair share.

Ding-a-ling-a-ling rang the handbell in the courtyard signalling the evening meal was over. Time was marching on. It seemed they would not eat that night after all. The mistress swooped in to inspect their handiwork.

"Well done. It seems you can follow instructions after all."

Perhaps it was the end of a long shift and the thought of putting her feet up with a sherry that made her more lenient? Or maybe it was her plan to terrify them until they became submissive, then ease up. No one really knew.

"Say your prayers, then get ready for bed. At eight o'clock sharp, the lights go out."

"Yes, miss," chorused the group quietly.

She handed each woman a nightshirt, as horrible, starched, and scratchy as their daytime uniforms, then closed the door, giving one final instruction.

"Settle down. I will be back to lock you in later."

Although Mabel had a new mattress, she didn't have a new pillow. Terrible stains covered the case of the one she had, and it was miserably thin. She used her pinafore to bolster the cushioning. However uncomfortable it was, she decided it would be preferable to what Ada would endure, lying with the dead bodies downstairs. She settled into position. The iron bed squeaked. Although she had not been found guilty, she felt that she was being punished just as harshly as her parents. The turning of the key in their door signalled the night time routine had begun.

With her immediate living arrangements finally resolved, naturally, her thoughts turned to Ruth and Joe and how they might cope during their first night in prison. She consoled herself that at least the people around her were not criminals. Well, not the bad sort, at least. Apart from that, she imagined the rest of their awful conditions to be the same. Guilt began to consume her. Maybe, if she had looked after Billy and Esther better, none of the Nithercotts would be facing a cold night alone. Endlessly ruminating, the chance of sleep seemed remote. She lost track of time, and eventually, the darkness consumed her tired mind.

The now-familiar clanging of the handbell at six o'clock signalled the mistress would soon be on her morning rounds. Gertrude explained that they had thirty minutes to dress in their uniforms, empty their chamber pots and prepare their beds for inspection.

"A little insider tip for you, the old woman advised. "Pour as much as you can into one or two pots, then get down to the privy quickly. The queue soon builds up. There's no time for extra trips."

Although the task would use up precious minutes, Mabel offered to go to the privy. She needed time to think. There was no guidance on the required standard or what would be scrutinised when it came to the inspection, leaving her to second guess. After receiving a scolding from the mistress the night before, the last thing she wanted to do was disappoint her a second time. In a blind panic, Mabel did her best to smooth down her mattress, then put her pillow squarely at the top of the bed. She turned back her basic grey blanket and hoped that would suffice. She didn't notice the other women had neat 'hospital corners' to their beds. Fortunately, her efforts were acceptable.

The bell rang again, and a male voice boomed 'breakfast'. Gertrude offered to lead them to the dining room.

> "Don't say a word on the way down there, or we'll be for the high jump. I don't know about you, but I'm starving after having no dinner last night. I don't want short rations."

Mabel noticed the seating was segregated into two distinct areas for men and women. A small serving hatch graced each entrance. The inmates looked more like machines than people as their arms scooped the gruel into their mouths repeatedly. For the old lags, any glimmer of humanity had long since been extinguished.

The mistress stood at the women's hatch, advising the server if the next person deserved a full or docked ration. Those with docked rations got a single hunk of bread. Those with a full one also received a pint of runny, grey gruel.

Ada Fairfax was nowhere to be seen.

Mabel's eye was drawn to a lady who foolishly objected to her docked ration. The mistress had a simple solution: give the woman nothing.

"There will be only punishments, no rewards," was the mantra she barked yet again.

"I hope Ada is alright," Mabel whispered to her room mates.

A split second later, she got a swift clip around the ear from one of the inmate wardens.

"You there. Leave your food and make your way to the oakum room."

Peggy stared in horror as Mabel was grabbed under the armpits and forced from the bench to her feet, then dragged out of the dining room so fast that her clogs barely touched the floor.

"Talking without permission, Miss," Mr McLaughlin explained as the cruel mistress glowered at the new girl.

Although the food looked awful, it did give some respite from grinding hunger. Mabel chastised herself for her foolishness. '*Why did I do that? You silly, silly girl. Today was going to drag as it is, without feeling hungry too.*'

She prayed she didn't forget another rule and make things even worse.

12

ESCAPING THE PUNISHMENT ROOM

In the punishment room, Mr McLaughlin gave Mabel her orders.

> "Take a length of tarred rope from the basket and split it down to its individual fibres. I expect you to complete five lengths by lunchtime."

The oakum didn't resemble the golden rope she'd seen on the rigging of a ship on the Thames. The wretched stuff was gnarled and blackened with a thick coating of rough goo, which stuck it together into one thick piece. No training was provided on how to split the awful stuff, forcing Mabel to watch another inmate hard at work. The woman grasped the oakum with her left hand, then, using her right, dug a hooked metal tool into the stiff strip and dragged it back towards her hip. The ebony coating cleaved in two. The process brought to mind slitting and gutting a fish. Bit by bit, several hundred golden fibres were liberated from their tarred casing. It was almost magical. The stiff oakum resembled long wavy lengths of a mermaid's flaxen hair once processed, and a single piece of it filled a half pail.

"Better get cracking, my girl. Watching me won't get your quota done," whispered the woman. "You'll learn more by having a go."

"Silence!" hissed the warden.

With the best bench seats by the light already taken, Mabel set to work in her dreary corner of the room. On the hour, the warden paced around the room, inspecting the contents of the buckets. Mabel's was the least filled by far.

"Come on, girl, be quick about it, else the mistress will put you in solitary."

The hook was difficult to force into the stiff cable. Mabel tried to coax the individual fibres into submission by hand. Soon, the area beneath her nails was agony as each one began to detach from her fingertips.

Later that morning, when doing his rounds, the governor struck up a conversation with her. It was customary for all new long-term inmates to be quizzed by the Board of Guardians, else the governor on arrival, under the pretence of trying to rehabilitate them. Mr Emsworth took the task more seriously than an average workhouse overseer.

"You are one of our new inmates from last night, aren't you—and you are being punished already?"

"Yes, Sir. Sorry, Sir," said Mabel, not knowing whether to look at him politely or to keep her eyes on her work.

"Leave that. Come to my office."

Everyone stared as Mabel skulked out to follow the master. On the first floor, his room was big and bright in comparison to her quarters. Large windows overlooked the flourishing workhouse allotment.

"No need to look so petrified—Miss—"

"Nithercott, Mabel Nithercott."

"It is part of the standard admission policy to question all inmates on arrival."

The disclosure did not help her relax. Being found in the punishment room so soon was sure to be a black mark?

"Now, tell me what happened. Your name sounds familiar, for some reason."

Tongue-tied, Mabel was unsure where to begin.

"Well then? Speak up."

"I spoke at breakfast, Sir."

"I didn't mean in the punishment room. I meant, why did a young girl like you end up in the workhouse? Are your parents dead?"

"No, Sir."

The governor sat tapping his two index fingers together under his chin as Mabel began to explain the family's meteoric fall from grace.

"—I did everything I could to assist them. I was dependable and hardworking. I completed all the housework. Pa was content for me to care for my brother at home. But, after Esther, my mother couldn't bring herself to trust me again. I did a lot to help Billy with his health issues, but it wasn't enough to persuade me ma, in the end."

He raised his hand to silence her.

"Enough."

"Sorry, Sir."

"Stop apologising every five minutes, for goodness' sake."

Mabel stood perfectly still and silent, like a guard on his first night watch.

"So, if I understand correctly, you took it upon yourself to help your family by making your own medicine."

The governor remembered where he heard the name.

"Ah yes, the Nithercott case. I remember now. According to the coroner's report, the treatment proved effective for the boy's superficial wounds at least."

"Yes, Sir. But—how did you?"

"One of my associates, the Reverend Bennett, was at the inquest and in court. He takes an interest in these matters."

These matters? The bewildered girl didn't move a muscle, thinking it best to leave the governor to his thoughts. His fingers tapped on the desk as he stared at his rows of books along the wall.

"Have you heard of Tynedale Hall, just off Commercial Road?"

The girl's brow furrowed.

"Well, the Reverend Bennett set it up. It is a new venture." Mr Emsworth explained. "We work together on philanthropic projects. Not everyone in a position of power wishes to exploit the poor or write them off. It is possible to lift the working class and help them better themselves if they are obedient and willing to accept help. Especially the younger inmates, like yourself, Miss Nithercott. The youngest people under our guardianship have industrial schools to turn to, but, at seventeen years of age, you are ineligible for such a place."

The master stood up and stared out of the window at the grey East End landscape beyond the perimeter wall.

"Although it makes me unpopular with the guardians, I am a different breed to their other governors. Like Dr Barnardo, I believe my Christian duty is to provide opportunities for youngsters who show me they can be loyal and dedicated workers. When these people are given a chance to secure work and gain independence, they contribute to the parish coffers rather than drain them. Unfortunately, our work has confirmed that it's too late to reform wayward adults, but for adolescents, our success rate for reformation is higher than the national average-- all thanks to Reverend Bennett's outstanding team."

Mabel thought there might be a domestic post for her at the hall. It sounded like a big operation. Hopefully, it would tide her over until Harry sorted something out at the telephone exchange?

"Your parents will be in prison for some time to come, which means I may have an opportunity for you. Thanks to the financial support of the reverend, our new public ward at St Olave's infirmary offers medical care to the local community and our inmates. The quality of our outpatient service has been praised by those behind Tynedale Hall. I'm determined to keep that good reputation. In addition, since members of the public pay for treatments, it helps offset the cost of care for the thousand-plus workhouse inmates."

Mabel looked bewildered.

"Last week, one of the trainee nurses turned up late for her shift in a drunken stupor. Completely unacceptable behaviour, of course. Sister Beresford dismissed her on the spot."

"And?"

"Given your natural aptitude for caring for the sick, you are of more use to me in the infirmary than the laundry. Since the union already provides your bed and board, it is an unpaid position, but it is a chance for advancement. Nursing is an excellent occupation for a woman."

Mabel couldn't believe her luck. The governor was nothing like the cruel mistress, determined to crush the soul out of the inmates. How fortunate she was to be under the stewardship of one of the few workhouse governors who believed that rehabilitation was more important than punishment. Male orphans had received vocational training and learned a trade for many years, thanks to Barnardo. Mr Emsworth and Reverend Bennett wanted to go a step further and assist more of Britain's young underclass to escape poverty, not just orphans.

"I trust there will be no discussion of this matter with the other inmates, particularly your cohorts, from yesterday evening. I recognised a few of the names. Most of them are women who prefer idling in the pub to self-improvement and professionalism. They deserve no nurturing."

"Yes, Sir. You have my word. Thank you. May I ask a question?"

He nodded.

"Why have you chosen to help me?"

"You misunderstand me, Miss Nithercott. This is not a case of favouritism, rather a practicality. The growing infirmary is short-staffed, and I have taken steps to deal with it. Your dedication to care provision was noted by the coroner. You have an aptitude for the work. Thus, I am prepared to give you a chance. But, be warned, do not let me down, else you will get your marching orders like the last trainee nurse."

"I won't let you down, Sir, I promise."

"See that you don't. I'll notify Sister Beresford to expect you in the inmates' ward following tomorrow's breakfast. Now, I suggest you get back to your oakum picking before the mistress finds you missing."

Mabel was lucky to be in such a new and progressive urban workhouse. Men like William Booth, the Methodist preacher and founder of the Salvation Army, had done a lot to shine a light on the plight of the poor. Unfortunately, rural workhouses were still very much more backward in their outlook.

Picking away with the hook, Mabel recalled Lydia's final words to her: 'Maybe some good will come out of this.' Perhaps, against all the odds, Lydia's prediction was accurate?

Excited and burdened by the secret, later, she spent another night lying awake in her bed. It wasn't just the weight of the opportunity that kept her up but also the constant groaning of her sick neighbours, the creaking of iron beds, and the rasping of smokers' wheezy lungs.

Her belly rumbled, she felt cold, but something inside her heart was aglow. She hoped with all her might that this could be the lucky break she desperately needed.

13

FIRST IMPRESSIONS

The morning bell rang out again. As the women tidied their beds, they discussed the day ahead.

"Bleedin' laundry for us," complained Peggy and Ada. "How about you, Gertrude?"

"Scrubbing floors. My poor old knees on those cold hard flagstones all day. It's not right," she wheezed, still struggling with a bad chest.

Hating having to lie, Mabel averted her gaze.

"I'm in the kitchen, I think. Anything would be preferable to yesterday's oakum picking!"

"Or sitting in solitary with a bunch of stiffs next door!" Ada lamented with a wry smile.

After another silent breakfast, on docked rations, Mabel sneaked to the inmates' infirmary. Over the coming weeks, she hoped she would demonstrate an aptitude for nursing. Everything the sister would tell her, she vowed to soak up like a sponge. The infirmary's healthcare protocols would be followed to the letter. She would be a model employee, albeit un-waged.

Her first day was nerve-racking. Before her shift be-gan, she stood on tiptoes by the ward's double doors and peered through the small glazed panel. The vast room was much larger and brighter than the rest of the workhouse, with plenty of tall windows that let in light. Along the longer walls, there were two rows of beds. She straightened her bonnet, then swung the door open.

"And you are?" boomed a voice.

A stern woman, Sister Beresford didn't suffer fools lightly.

"Miss Nithercott," Mabel said with a curtsey. "Mr Emsworth said you would be expecting me?"

"Ah, the new inmate helper. The golden rule of nursing is to keep things clean. I am sure making a bed is not beyond you, even at this early stage. Your first task will be to change the sheets—this is critical if disease is not to spread."

"Yes, Miss."

"You will address me as 'Sister Beresford', or simply, 'sister.'"

"Yes, Sister Beresford," Mabel replied, head bowed, and one knee bent.

Once again, she got her ears chewed.

"For goodness' sake, stop curtseying. Anyone
would think I was the queen! Make yourself
useful. Go to the store cupboard over there
and collect some fresh bedding."

Mabel's head spun round on her shoulders like an
owl's as she looked for the door.

"People think all nurses do is give patients
foul-tasting medicines three times a day,
then laze at a desk. There's a lot more to it
than that, Miss Nithercott, as you'll soon discover. Now, hurry up. Sheets, dear girl!"

Mabel hurried back with an armful of linen and
placed it on a nearby trolley.

"We'll start at this end of the ward and work
our way along."

Sister Beresford took the corners of a sheet and
opened it with a vigorous flap of her arms.

"Miss Nithercott, this is Mr Harris. He prefers
to be addressed as Edward."

"Sir," she greeted with another nervous curtsey.

She snapped her knees straight under the sister's icy
glare.

"Do you mind if we use you for practice, Edward?"

She continued before he agreed, whipping back his grey blanket like a matador twirls a cape.

"Edward was a carpenter before he fell on hard times, weren't you?"

"Yes, my four sons went off to the Middle East to fight in the Anglo-Egyptian war. Left me on my own, they did. Little rotters. When I was too old to work, I fell behind on the rent and ended up here. Looking back, I should have had a daughter, or got myself a new young wife. Got them to care for me," he chuckled. "I believe Sister Beresford has had some army experience?"

"Yes. Father was an officer in The Crimea. I trained at the Royal Victoria, a British field hospital for the wounded men who returned home. I had many happy years there."

"How did you end up here, sister?" asked Mabel.

"A happy accident, I suppose. Tynedale was looking for a ward sister to run the new public wing, and so I applied. Reverend Bennett does so much good work here in Whitechapel. He's even organised a partnership with Cambridge University, so those posh medical and legal students can live and work here. Trial by fire for those Eton types, I expect." she joked. "I'm confident they've never witnessed anything like what goes on around the East End. Isn't that right, Edward?"

Harris smirked as Sister Beresford spun her hand over, signalling for him to roll to the far edge of the mattress.

"We shall change the patient's sheets whilst he remains in situ."

"Yes, sister."

"Now, move the pillow up. Get it under his head."

Mabel took a breath and made the adjustment in a single, bold move.

"Excellent. We now fold the old soiled sheet towards the patient to clear the mattress for the fresh one, which we lay alongside like this."

Mabel stared at the gruesome stains on the mattress. What on earth caused marks like that? Suddenly, the aggravation of making a fresh mattress on her first night seemed far less burdensome.

"I dare say your roommates working in the laundry will be sewing us a batch of new covers this week. We try to change them once a month if we can. Now smooth the new sheet out. We don't want any wrinkles. Causes bed-sores."

Mr Harris rolled back onto the clean sheet as the soiled one was removed and thrown in the laundry cart. Sister Beresford smoothed down the fresh linen and pulled the grey blanket back up around Edward's shoulders.

"There. All done."

"I feel like royalty." muttered Mr Harris. "Forget Albert, I'm King Edward VII of England now."

"Yes, of course, you are," replied Sister Beresford dismissively. "Now, Mabel, please attend to the rest of the patients' beds. We are understaffed today. Another nurse should be here, but I've heard she's been placed in solitary confinement for a violent outburst. I shall have to have words with Mr Emsworth about her. I keep being given imbecile inmates since they are not suited to more dangerous work in the kitchens or laundry. I cannot operate in such chaos."

Mabel wondered why so many of the nurses were so unreliable. Was it that the work was so hard, the ward sisters were so strict, or that the trainees were so undisciplined? She vowed not to put a foot wrong—ever. Eager to impress the sister, she got to work on the beds straight away. After a rocky start, it got easier the more she did. Within ninety minutes, she had finished.

"All done, Sister Beresford."

"Good. This morning, I trust you have learned, Miss Nithercott, that nursing entails putting patients in a state of wellbeing, where Mother Nature is aided in her efforts to heal them. A nurse should be concerned about everything that her patients are concerned about. We are their companions and caregivers, as well as their support and attendants. We are there first thing in the morning, broom in hand, sweeping and dusting quickly and quietly. Then we assist with each individual toilet. Finally, breakfast is served."

Mabel felt her brain fill to capacity then overflow with the onslaught of information.

"After that, we clean up the crockery and remove the breadcrumbs. Then there's bedmaking, which, as you can see, is a tricky task when a ward has up to fifteen bedridden patients. Workhouse inmates only get the most basic of care, but there is more provision in the public ward: the application of poultices or dressings, the charting of temperatures, the rubbing in of liniments, and other medical directions, all of which must all be executed with care. In tandem, the patient's paperwork must be completed in a timely fashion. The inspectors and medical officers insist our case notes are sufficiently detailed and in good order. There is little money available for medicine for the inmates. However, the guardians like to keep the mortality rate down and will consider paying for treatments as a last resort."

Over the next few days, Mabel soaked up everything taught, returning to the drudgery of bedpans and vomit between her tuition without a hint of complaint. She did all she could to demonstrate she had an aptitude for nursing. For Sister Beresford, her unwavering diligence was a breath of fresh air, and she gleefully advised Mr Emsworth: 'Miss Nithercott is unlikely to end up in solitary confinement like the others.'

Mabel's cheerful bedside manner endeared her to the patients, and they enjoyed her company. In time, Augusta Fishwick, another elderly patient, noticed a young delivery man taking a shine to Mabel. His covert habit of gazing at her with a twinkle in his eye gave him away. With Sister Beresford busy in the public ward, Mrs Fishwick beckoned the man over. Mabel was engrossed in clipping her patient's talon-like toenails. The fidgeting made her wonder what the woman was up to.

"Mabel, this is young Mr Stanford."

"Good afternoon," the two greeted in blushing unison.

"Archie's father owns a pharmacy in Blackheath."

"Yes, he does," Archie confirmed, just before Augusta started teasing him.

"According to reports, Charles Stanford was awarded the contract because he is an old school friend of Mr Ensworth's. I'm sure it's worth a pretty penny that little deal. Archie delivers something almost every day."

"Shush now, Mrs Fishwick. My father won the work because his bid was the cheapest. You know the guardians. Any excuse to penny pinch, and they will."

The young man's face reddened further.

"Please excuse me; I have to leave. There's a wagon full of supplies still to be unloaded, and they won't deliver themselves."

*

From that day on, Archie made a point of smiling at Mabel every time he saw her. Not only did the kind act bring cheer to the young woman's face, but she also felt a slight tingling in her stomach. She dared not speak to him, though, terrified of disappointing her superiors. The governor had warned her that one wrong move and her infirmary opportunity would be over. Neglecting her duties to fraternise with male suppliers felt very much like a wrong move. The best she could do was smile and hopefully strike up a conversation with him and Sister Beresford should the situation present itself.

At night, back in her dormitory with the others, she felt very lucky indeed. All they had to look forward to was backbreaking manual labour. After a few weeks of forced work, Peggy and Ada announced their plan to leave the workhouse and take their chances on the outside.

"We're going to hang around some pubs. Ask about and see if any of the guys have any, err, 'needs' we can meet. We'll soon get enough for a coffin bed for a week or two, then see where we end up."

Gertrude was the next to leave--via the dead room. Pneumonia took her.

Mabel kept herself to herself in the dormitory but did eventually confess she was helping in the infirmary. Lying about being in the kitchen had been exhausting. Furthermore, the constant rotation of inmates assigned to every part of the workhouse meant that her deception would be discovered sooner or later. No one liked a liar in their midst.

Simeon Bennett settled back into the armchair in Mr Emsworth's office after returning from his latest meeting at Tynedale.

"The meeting to discuss the women from the Christian mission visiting the orphans on Sundays has gone well. And there has been progress on the concept of the professional library," he reported. "The guardians are utterly resistant, of course. I keep reminding them it is easier for us to find work for inmates when they keep their skills sharp and up to date, rather than locking them in here until they rot away, but they never see it that way."

"Quite," said Emsworth . "   Can I tempt you in a little afternoon tipple, my good man?"

"Oh, go on then. I could do with one," the reverend replied with a grin. "I'm rushed off my feet these days. Too many projects, too little time, I fear. Speaking of projects, how is Miss Nithercott performing?"

"Very well, Simeon. Very well indeed. Our infirmary experiment seems to have been a success. I have high hopes for the girl. Sister, too, is most impressed."

Mr Emsworth's smiled faded when he added:

"Then again, since the last imbecile nurse nearly scalded a baby to death, the performance bar is rather low."

"We knew it would take time to raise standards in the inmate infirmary, Douglas, but we shall prevail. Have faith! I will speak to Miss Nithercott on my next visit to the ward."

"Another whisky, Simeon?"

"Best not. More blasted meetings this evening. I have a team of fifty, and yet I am more overworked than ever. Must dash."

Downstairs in the infirmary, Mabel awaited the start of her first night shift in the infirmary, worrying she wouldn't have Sister Beresford's steadying hand nearby.

"Stop fidgeting, Nithercott. I think you have the makings of a fine nurse, else I wouldn't have adjusted the rota, would I? Your conduct on your probationary period has been exemplary."

"Yes, sister. I will continue to do my best. You will be proud, I promise."

"Good. Or I'll be onto you like a ton of bricks!"

The man sitting at Mr Harris's bedside stood up to join the conversation.

"Hello, Reverend Simeon Bennett," he said, extending his hand to the girl. "I admire your work ethic, Miss Nithercott. High motives are a much-needed quality in a hospital nurse. I fear the trials are as numerous as the blessings. Patients, being ill, are prone to fretfulness. Their manners are left lacking on occasion. They can't help being tetchy, I suppose—"

He leaned in and whispered:

"—but, between you and me, I am sure some are deliberately rude and ungrateful, don't you think?"

"A little perhaps," she confessed, "although I can only speak for the inmate patients."

"It's such a worthy but demanding career for a woman. A nurse must harden her heart to become accustomed to the sight of pain. She must hold vigils by deathbeds and witness the grief of the living. It may fall to her to massage a dislocated joint back in position, cauterise a raw wound, or otherwise cause suffering in the pursuit of a cure."

"Nothing so glamorous for me, though. I spend most of my time changing beds, reverend," confessed Mabel.

"I am sure you will pass from those simple to more complex duties. Sister Beresford will only lay responsibility on your shoulders when you are ready. You will go on from strength to strength as you wrestle, fight and pray because the path you will tread is indeed a glorious one."

The words warmed Mabel's soul. Simeon turned to Beresford.

"Well, I must be getting on, sister. As always, I have a myriad of things to do back at Tynedale."

"See you next week, reverend?" she said before marching towards the public ward. "Please excuse me. I have my final rounds to do."

"So, you are covering the night shift tonight, Miss Nithercott?"

"Yes. My first one."

"Here's something to pass the time if the patients nod off later. Don't let sister see this." he warned, slipping her his newspaper. "As a nurse, reading, keeping in touch with the wider world is important. Especially since you're so far away from it here."

"But I am only an inmate helper, reverend, not a trainee," Mabel corrected.

He put his finger to his lips, delighted by her modest honesty.

"Shhh. Wait and see, Miss Nithercott. Wait and see."

Unused to praise, Mabel bowed her head awkwardly. Bennett made his way towards the exit as the girl fumbled to conceal the newspaper in the folds of her skirt.

"Reverend! Stop!" barked Sister Beresford.

Mabel panicked. Why did she accept the newspaper? She thought she was done for.

"Reverend—that's the linen cupboard door—not the exit!"

Noticing his mistake, the sheepish cleric reappeared.

"It's been a long week, sister," he chuckled.

"So it has, reverend," sister sympathised, her arms burdened with a large stack of outpatient notes.

Seeing sister engrossed in her work at the head nurse's desk, Mabel tiptoed into the linen store, seeking a good spot to conceal the paper. After weeks of confinement, no Sunday visitors, nor Peggy, Ada, or Gertrude to talk to, it was a treat too important to miss. She vowed to bide her time and only look at the paper in the dead of night when it was safe. Beresford came to check on her. Mabel nearly jumped out of her skin. *'Did she see?'*

"Right. That's everything straight for today's shift. I shall be off. If there is a problem, you are to ask the night porter to come for me immediately. Is that clear?"

"Yes, I am to call the night porter," she confirmed. "Everything will be fine; you can leave it to me. You're exhausted. Now, please get some rest."

As expected, Mabel made sure everyone who wanted some received their ration of bread and soup. She checked on each patient, shared a kind word with each one, emptying their bedpans or chamber pots, then dimmed the gaslights in the ward. Like Nightingale before her, by oil lamp, she settled down to update the notes, Beresford's warning the medical officer took a dim view of any gaps in patient records echoing in her mind. It was only when her administrative work was complete, that she noticed Sister Beresford had put a copy of Honnor Morten's book "Dictionary of Essential Nursing Skills" in the desk drawer.

She licked her lips as her index finger skimmed along the table of contents, deciding which topic to delve into. There was so much to absorb! The first thing she reviewed was how to deal with blocked airways, the ailment that had taken poor Esther to meet her maker. She stumbled over the pronunciation of the word Heimlich. Luckily for Mabel, there were a series of clear diagrams explaining the manoeuvre and the steps were soon etched in her mind.

Reading until her brain could take no more, she would have a thousand questions for sister when she saw her again. Enthralled by the material, the time flew. Glancing up at the wall clock, she flinched. Eleven-thirty! She was late for her observations.

As she paced along the aisle, thankfully, all the patients were either sound asleep or dozing comfortably. Alone, in the dark dead of night, Mabel could hear the newspaper calling out to her. She looked around. The night porter was elsewhere, so she slipped into the storeroom and teased the newspaper from its hiding place.

Once unfurled, the broadsheet covered the little desk. The young woman's eyes scanned the front page. Below the headline, was an equally prominent advertisement. The product name made Mabel's teeth grind.

CORNELIUS SPEAKS

"No one has the right to dogmatics in medicine, which is still an inexact science." Sir Thomas McKenzie.

Thrilling testimony

listen and learn what the people of Middlesbrough say.

QUIMBY'S EMBROCATION 2s. Per Tub. Sold Every-where.

To the Sick and the Lame; to all Suffer-ing from Chronic Diseases; to the Incurables; and those whom Doctors have Failed to Relieve; to those whose life is Misery on Account of Constant Pain and Suffering

—NOW IS YOUR, OPPORTUNITY. READ AND REMEMBER—

QUIMBY'S REMEDIES Are now univer-sally acknowledged to be the Best of all Household Remedies. The Chemists eve-rywhere say there never were Medicines which gave Greater Satisfaction, which had such   large and phenomenal sales.

They CURE INDIGESTION and all Stom-ach Diseases, BILIOUSNESS and all Liver Complaints, CONSTIPATION and all Dis-orders of the Bowels, DROPSY and most Kidney Troubles RHEUMATISM and RHEUMATIC GOUT in all their forms, LUMBAGO. SCIATIC BACKACHE, HEAD-ACHE, NEURALGIA, and DEPRESSION of SPIRITS. They REMOVE all IMPURITIES the BLOOD

DIRECTIONS ACCOMPANY EACH CURE SOLD

SEE THAT THE NAME QUIMBY IS EMBOSSED ON
EVERY TIN

Dear sir,

With pleasure, I sent you a testimonial concerning the curative effect of your remedies. I gave one instance, out of the many, a poor widow aged 72 for a long period suffered intensely with her right knee and could not put her foot to the ground without pain, as if a knife were piercing it. Often, she could neither sleep at night nor scarcely get out by day. However, having applied your remedies, she can now walk with ease and comfort. This is the only case out of one of many, which have come to my special attention. You, sir, are at liberty to make what you please of this.

I am dear sir, truly yours, Reverend Richard Nichols Free Methodist Minister, 7, Cambridge Terrace, Middlesbrough.

TAKE CARE THAT IT DOES NOT PASS YOU BY.

It has been in Newcastle, Sunderland, South Shields, Middlesbrough, and other cities, so it will be in the South. But, in these difficult days, a wise man takes nothing for granted and believes nothing unless it be

**undoubtedly true and well authenti-
cated.**

I write in thanks. The following testimony is authen-
tic and will bear investigation. It needs no comment
but speaks for itself to the efficacy. I have been suffering from glandular swellings for twelve years. I'm
glad to say I'm at work again this week and on the
night shift. I do not know how to thank you enough.
I hope you will be rewarded for it at some future
time, please make use of this what you will.

Yours truly, William Croft, Gateshead, aged 43

'Pure balderdash!'

The effect was marvellous. While suffering from a violent attack of lumbago, I was advised to try your
remedy and did so. The effect was marvellous. I ob-
tained almost immediate relief, and in two days, the
pain entirely left me, and I am happy to state I have
been perfectly pain-free ever since,

Yours respectfully, Our Organising Agent, the Walls-
end Temperance Society, Quimby Limited.

*'He's even got his own salesmen writing in. They're
hardly going to say it's useless, are they?'*

Mabel turned to the second page, hoping to find
more positive news. A new mainline station was set
to open, paving the way for new express routes to the
Southend-on-Sea. As soon as Harry got her the job at

the telephone exchange, she planned to take the three of them on a day trip. It would be lovely in summer. Mabel's mind drifted off: ice creams, the little bathing huts by the crystal blue water, donkey rides on the sandy beach, puffing paddle steamers and glorious piers.

Her reverie was disturbed by the sound of violent convulsions, making her jump to her feet. It was poor Mrs Fishwick. Mabel did her best to restrain the woman and diagnose what was wrong. The old woman's head was bent back as far back as it would go. Her skeletal hands clutched at the bedsheets, and her feet kicked wildly at nothing. Apart from that, there was no sound.

In a panic, Mabel looked in the corridor for the night porter, but he'd vanished. Any hopes of alerting Sister Beresford were dashed. What was she to do?

By now, several of the inmate patients had been awakened by the kerfuffle, with several standing around the bed. Mabel racked her brains. Then, there it was, the flash of inspiration she needed. Mrs Fishwick was tiring. The young woman put her ear to her gaping mouth. There was no sound, and no hot air against her cheek. Sweeping the denture-less mouth with her index finger, Mabel found a large chunk of stale bread wedged at the back of her throat. Of course! Mrs Fishwick had hidden some bread for a midnight snack.

"Come on, old girl, let's get you better," Mabel whispered in her ear.

Guided by her photographic recollection of Honnor Morton's illustration, she picked up Mrs Fishwick from behind, raised her up and gave her ribcage an almighty upward and inward heave. The bread shot out of her mouth like a cannonball.

"Thank you!" gasped Mrs Fishwick, gripping the girl's hand tightly.

"Jolly good show, Mabel," cheered Mr Harris! "I do believe you have saved Ethel's life!"

There was a ripple of applause from the shadowy little crowd that had gathered around the bed. Mabel was bursting with pride; she had defeated the ailment that had taken her sister, which gave her some comfort. It was then the ward doors swung open, and the night porter finally returned.

"What's happened? Shall I get Sister Beresford?"

"That won't be necessary, Mr Hammerton. Edith will be right as rain after a good cup of sugary tea." Mr Harris advised. "Isn't that right, darlin'."

Edith gave a relieved but toothless smile. Mabel was discovering there was a lot more to being a nurse than teasing out a splinter from an angry thumb and filling in observation papers. The realisation there would be no warning when someone would be in dire need hit her hard. Faultless decisive action was needed each, and every time.

'I do hope I am cut out for this. What if I was just lucky today?'

14

UNWELCOME
UPDATES

Days turned into weeks, and weeks turned into months at the workhouse. Each Sunday, she hoped for the promised visit from Mrs Kirkham--or Harry--but there were none. Despite the increasing loneliness, it cheered the girl to know her progress in the ward was stellar and that she was held in high esteem after the incident with Mrs Fishwick. Sister Beresford was also delighted not to be lumbered with lazy inmates that the cook and laundress had tried to foist on someone else. She gave Mabel more responsibility, and she thrived. Any time the young woman got stuck, Honnor Morton's raft of textbooks had the answers. The sister had a sneaking suspicion it would soon be time to allocate the newcomer to the public ward.

"Mr Harris's bed sores on his heels are worsening, sister. What should we do?"

"We need to relieve the pressure on them. Also, keeping the open wounds clean from any discharge will stop them deteriorating further. Infected and dead tissue will need debridement."

The new term flummoxed Mabel.

"Debriding, it's very simple. We flush the wound and scrape out dead and dying tissue. Then we dress it with an antiseptic balm, gauze, and bandages. We are running low on the balm, and there is no money to buy more for the inmates. So, we'll have to make do with brine or iodine."

"My brother had a similar skin complaint. I concocted a homemade remedy with some freely-growing plants, paraffin, and a few other things. It is cheap to prepare."

"I see. Tell me more."

Mabel took a chance.

"Well, rather than tell you, we could try it. I brought a small container of it with me when I fled the family home. It's in inmate storage. Could you ask Mr Emsworth for a special dispensation and get it for me? I think it will be good for Mr Harris's sores."

Sister mulled over the proposition but left without sharing her conclusion. Later, as Mabel checked the list of mid-morning medicines, she felt someone beside her. It was the governor, his face drawn and solemn.

"Ah, there you are. I have an important matter to discuss with you."

"Me, Sir?"

"Yes, You, Nithercott. Now."

'Argh! Has sister told him of my request for the balm?'

"Sister, I will bring Miss Nithercott back, forthwith, once this troubling turn of events has been dealt with."

The nurse's face took on the same solemn countenance, adding to Mabel's fears. The governor strode ahead as he escorted her to his office, Mabel having to break into a trot to keep up. Mr Emsworth closed the door and settled into his leather desk chair.

"Is this about asking for the balm, sir? I didn't think you would mind?"

"Balm? What balm? No, Miss Nithercott, it's your mother. She's due to be released from prison very soon, probably next week. Rather than having the two of you here, I expect the union to give you a small out-of-pocket payment to help you both find your feet. I'm guessing she'll come and get you. You will need to make your own living arrangements once you have been reunited. I doubt you'd want to be separated from each other in this house. There is a refuge in Fulham provided for prisoner rehabilitation which helps with

domestic service tuition and placements,
which is available to you. It must have been a
trying time for your mother. She'll need to be
looked after."

Mr Emsworth looked out of the window as he delivered the killer blow.

"Once you leave the house, with regret, your
nursing instruction will come to an end. I
have to find another inmate to take over
your unpaid duties."

Inside, Mabel was panicking. How would she help her ma without her father's assistance? It was a formidable question. Worse, putting her mother first meant saying goodbye to her informal apprenticeship in the infirmary. It made her feel sick just thinking about it. Marking the painful days until her mother was released, she busied herself with her work, hoping something miraculous would happen.

'Please, just let me get what I deserve for once in my life! '

15

LATE NIGHT WANDERING

Locked up alone in a harsh Holloway prison cell, Ruth Nithercott's mental state had deteriorated dramatically as she was subjected to a series of disciplinary procedures designed to make female prisoners more malleable to reform. Women needed saving twice, firstly from their criminality and then from their deviance from expected female behaviour. Barely a week after her sentence began, Holloway's prison superintendent had written to the Director of Her Majesty's Convict Prisons about Ruth's 'lunacy.' She had become 'so outrageously violent', having 'used base language, assaulted a fellow prisoner, smashed several window panes and torn up her clothes in fits of temper', that she was required to wear a straitjacket. The superintendent requested that she be transferred to Bethlem Royal Hospital, Southwark, better suited to help patients with mental problems, but refused. Released from solitary confinement, she returned to lengthy periods of forced labour, remaining apprehensive, volatile, and vulnerable to irritability and depression.

The warden unlocked Ruth Nithercott's door.

"Time for you to go, Number 4629."

The door squealed open, and the warden directed Ruth to the left. The prison passages were long, narrow, and white as snow thanks to many thick coats of lime. From the monotony of their colour and simple arrangement, they seemed to be positively endless. Each cell door was fitted with the same tiny metal escutcheon, perfect for spying on the occupant. Beneath lay the huge ugly lock, typical of older prisons. The cells in this section of the building were like defensive casements in naval forts, except that their roofs were not vaulted. Instead, the main atrium for each wing had narrow windows along the length of the ceiling, letting in some natural light.

Eventually, Ruth arrived at the little old-fashioned porter's office to the side of the main gates. There she was met by the principal matron, who was saluted in military style by the prison gatekeeper on her arrival.

The possessions the prisoner arrived with were dumped on a table—her bundled up clothing and the sling she used to transport Billy on that final fateful day of false freedom. Stunned, the vivid reminder of her precious son's short life grabbed her throat and took her breath.

"Oi! Did you hear me? Get changed, Nithercott. Are you being awkward on purpose?"

Still stood like a bewildered rabbit, two strong hands shoved Ruth in the direction of a hessian curtain, throwing her clothes after her. She took off the stiff prison uniform and put on her tatty civilian clothes. Images buzzed through her mind—the argument at home, the trip to the knacker's yard, Miss Wilmot in Clerkenwell, the market. In her pocket, her fingers brushed against two of the shillings Ethel Wilmot had given her for Hercules's bowl. The third was pilfered by an unscrupulous prison officer months ago, on the afternoon of her arrival.

"Hurry up."

Ruth shuffled from behind the curtain towards the desk, clutching her uniform.

"I'm ready to go," she mumbled, not believing a word of it.

The uniform was whisked under the desk as the newly-liberated woman was led through a smaller door embedded in the left of the two massive iron gates that formed the main entrance. It shut behind her with a loud clang, followed by the clanks of some bolts slid back into locking position. Stood outside the prison, she wondered which was the quickest way to get to the workhouse.

The grieving mother had found her time in prison a harrowing and demoralising experience. She had not adjusted well, left alone to brood on the death of her two children and the probable failure of her marriage. After all, it was her stubborn foolishness that had got him a year in Newgate. Her admission to the Fulham rehabilitation facility had already been denied due to her bad behaviour. Inmates told her the next best option was to seek refuge at the Deserving Women's Christian Mission, open to wiping the slate clean and helping offenders. Ruth did not feel like an offender, and the word jarred with her. She still believed she was a caring, albeit cursed, mother. If the mission was full, St Olave's Workhouse would be the next most likely stop on the road to rock bottom. But Ruth Nithercott seldom did what was expected of her.

It was a warm, summery afternoon, one of those ideal times for a leisurely stroll through Victoria Park, but the ex-convict found the atmosphere to be dark and oppressive. The dazzling reintroduction into Civvy Street, with its bustling lanes of food seller stalls, pungent smells, fiery flames, and hoarse voices barking about their wares, overwhelmed the poor woman's brain.

Confused, instead of heading south-east along the busy Holloway Road, the most direct route to the mission, she headed south, towards Blackfriars. As she shambled along in her thick winter clothes, trance-like, she invited a sea of cruel stares. With a dipped head, her unfocused gaze fell to the floor, a few feet ahead of her. In her pocket, her fingers continued to tumble the two shillings over and over, clinging to the only piece of security she had left in her miserable existence.

*

Back at the workhouse, Sister Beresford was examining Mr Harris's heels, where the worst of his bedsores had formed.

"Well, I must say Miss Nithercott, the salve has stopped the infection in its tracks. There is no new tissue to debride. Very impressive. I think we should make more and do a proper trial. I shall speak to the governor. If the bulk of the ingredients can be gathered for free, I am sure he will think it feasible to make a batch of our own. Perhaps we can have a Sunday outing to gather the materials? I shall speak to Simeon the next time he comes to read to the patients. He might be able to organise a charabanc trip."

"I feel honoured, sister. I would be delighted to help."

Mr Harris inspected his feet, then pretended to do a jig as he lay in his bed, singing the chorus of 'The Daring Young Man on the Flying Trapeze' at full volume.

"Be quiet this instant, Mr Harris," snapped the sister. "We have patients here who need their bedrest."

"But I am practicing for my music hall career! All the best performers practice! I'll be as good as George Leybourne soon. This is another belter of a tune."

> *I went to see a young lady*
> *I've been there before*
> *Her shoes and stockings in her hand*
> *And her feet all over the floor*
> *Champagne Charlie is my name*
> *And rogueing n' stealing is a game*

Sister was furious as she towered over him at his bedside.

"Heavens! Not this again. You are a crippled carpenter, not 'Champagne Charlie', Mr Harris. Please, calm down. This racket is impressing no one. Have you lost your grip on reality, man?"

In protest, Edward snarled and drew his grey blanket over his head. Seeing Beresford's ire reminded Mabel not to disappoint her. She hoped that this Sunday would be the Sunday Mrs Kirkham finally visited. Her knowledge of the balm recipe had grown sketchy with time.

*

Ruth walked past The Castle pub, stopping briefly to look through the front window, before turning down the dark alleyway alongside. She gave an insistent knock on the outdoor serving hatch.

"A quart of gin, please," she murmured.

"Right you are, love. You look like you could do with this," said the buxom barmaid, leaning to collect the money. "I only drink on days that begin with 'T,' so Tuesdays, Thursdays, today, and tomorrow," she added with a chirpy giggle that was not reciprocated.

Ruth yanked the stopper from the bottle. Having not drunk for months, the spirit was potent. The grog burned her throat, and the odour stung her nose like mustard in a sandwich. Oppressive thoughts circled in her head: Billy. Esther. Mabel. Joe. Billy. Esther. Mabel. Joe.

Increasingly out of touch with her surroundings, she staggered off towards the main thoroughfare, leaving the barmaid to shout, 'Oi! What about my jug?' as it slipped out of her fingers and smashed on the flagstones.

Soon, Ruth found herself tottering along the Thames embankment, close to Blackfriars. Armed with a second jug of gin, she raised the bottle to her lips and drank the last dregs before barging into a group of labourers chatting and smoking on their one night out.

"You alright, luv?"

There was no reply.

"Silly tart."

Blackfriars' Bridge was bustling with wagons carrying goods to and from the neighbouring railway stations. Throngs of people crisscrossed it too, some eager to finish their punishing shifts, others dreading starting theirs. Labourers staggered towards the next bar or pie and mash shop. Costers and artists set up their carts along the low walls, pinning their wares to their display boards. Shoe-shine boys invited well-dressed gentlemen to take a seat for a moment. Heavy omnibuses trundled by. Ruth became increasingly isolated as the liquor wrapped around her brain, snuffing out any glimmer of lightness in her thoughts.

Amid the chaos, no one noticed the poor woman stumbling to the edge of the stony precipice. Swirling eddies and ripples formed behind the bridge supports as the perilous tidal flow dragged the Thames kicking and screaming towards the North Sea. Menacing to the watermen, the dark depths appealed to many tortured women, compelling them to stare transfixed into the abyss. Just like them, Ruth felt the only way out of the agony, the solution to the insurmountable pain, was for her to throw herself into oblivion before anyone could stop her. The horrific splash alerted a waiting shoe-shine boy, who signalled the watermen for help a split-second later.

"Look sharpish, lads! There's a woman down there!"

Ruth's thin arms flailed above the water. The winter clothing quickly became waterlogged and began dragging her down into the dark depths of the river. John Deering, the nearest of the boatmen, rowed across, his gaze fixed on the splashes. He recalled warnings about this kind of rescue from his father and didn't want to get too close if the thrashing woman grabbed his tiny hull and flipped it over.

"Help me, Vincent," Deering yelled as the man plunged the oars deep into the water and yanked them back, his arms at full stretch.

The two men tried everything to get her head out of the water, and eventually, as she tired, they could lift her face to safety. Ruth was dragged on to a small jetty, where she lay motionless. Listening for breathing, they discovered it was too late.

"Get a copper, Vin!" John ordered. The worried man ran off faster than a bolting horse. Now alone, Deering, the devious boatman, rummaged through her belongings and smiled as he found two shiny shillings, which he tucked into his own pockets.

The anonymous woman was pronounced dead at the scene. It would take several days to figure out the victim's identity. Struggling women jumping into raging rivers was an all-too-common occurrence: a spurned marriage proposal, an illicit pregnancy, an abusive husband. So many reasons triggered such a deep melancholia and such desperate remedial measures.

In such circumstances, the deceased's description was circulated to the papers, prisons, and work-houses, and more often than not, someone would come forth with a suitable name.

Despite Ruth's formal identification, the institutions were unaware that her daughter was a St Olave's res-ident. Mr Emsworth would be the one to suss out the sad connection.

"It seems you will be with us a little longer, Miss Nithercott," he said in an attempt to sof-ten the blow.

He let her read the newspaper article for herself, but still, the news broke her heart. In less than a year, a third Nithercott family member had passed away. She could have been forgiven for rounding the total up to four. Her father was as good as dead too. She had heard nothing from him whatsoever, not even a visiting order request since his imprisonment. The only upside was that she would not be expected to join her mother in the mission, giving her a little longer to carry on with her nursing instruction.

Mabel folded the paper and returned it to the gover-nor, wiping a tear from her cheek. If she had only turned the page, she would have seen a tiny feature revealing Honnor Morton's associate, Eliza Twining, philanthropic daughter of the wealthy tea dynasty, was funding nursing scholarships for the underprivileged.

*

News of Mabel's loss travelled quickly through the workhouse. Some people were sympathetic. Others took pleasure in her pain, particularly the joyless porter, Mr McLaughlin, who never seemed to like anyone or anything. Mabel thought it best to keep herself busy by tending to her inmate patients, hoping that she would soon be trusted enough to be transferred to the public wing. To hasten that transition, she was eager to resume work on her antiseptic skin balm. Sister Beresford had agreed that the results from the trial on Edward Harris had been promising. It seemed her best hope for progression.

Recently, Edward's temperament had deteriorated, and changing his dressings had become more of a chore. Rather than cantankerousness, Sister Beresford suspected senility was the root cause of his problematic behaviour and planned to discuss his mental state with the medical officer at his next inspection.

The curmudgeonly fellow refused to sit still and delighted in yelling all manner of abuse at the women as they cared for him. Then, during one of these fraught sessions, Mabel heard a terrible commotion in the storeroom, which stopped her in her tracks. What on earth was that?

"Please excuse me, Mr Harris."

Fuming, Harris directed a rambling string of obscenities at her as she went to investigate. She ignored him. As she rounded the storeroom corner, she discovered Archie sprawled on the floor next to his trolley, buried under a landslide of toppled shelving and medical supplies. Although shaken, he seemed to be unhurt.

"Here, let me help you!"

"You don't have to, Mabel."

"I know, but I don't want you to get into trouble. Besides, this will take an age to tidy up on your own."

Archie repaired the damaged storage unit, and together, they put the things back on the shelves.

"I hope I'm not speaking out of turn, Mabel, but I saw the article--"

"--article?" she questioned.

"--in the newspaper--about your mother. I'm so sorry. If there's anything I can do, you must tell me."

Mabel, too upset to speak, busied herself tidying a heap of splints.

"Forgive me. I shouldn't have brought it up."

He changed the subject swiftly.

"You seem to be doing well with your nursing here. My father says that sister is pleased with you."

"Thank you."

"I saw something else of interest in the paper too."

"Yes?"

"I believe that Reverend Bennett has been raising money to set up a vocational library here in the workhouse. He's such a powerhouse for good, isn't he, that man? Very different to a lot of the other folk around here. All they seem to do is look down on the people who are struggling in life."

"I think access to books will be a real blessing, Archie. One of the ladies from the mission dropped off a nursing guide for sister, and I found it invaluable."

"Miss Nithercott, come here this instant!" hollered Sister Beresford, sounding louder than an artillery sergeant-major.

"Mr Harris still needs a fresh dressing applying. What are you thinking wandering off like that?"

"Coming!"

"I better go," Mabel whispered with a smile.

*

The weekend arrived, and Mabel received word that she would have her first official Sunday guest—at last, the stars had aligned, and Lydia Kirkham planned to pay a visit. Tittle-tattle about Ruth's death had spread like wildfire through Prospect Street and formed the catalyst for Lydia to finally leave the house.

Mabel entered the visiting area and made her way to her old friend sitting in the far corner.

> "You're really here. It's so good to see you." Mabel trilled, "But, I have to confess, you look peaky?"

> "That's because I am, my dear. Terrible trouble with my lungs. Pneumonia, they reckon. Couldn't get out of my pit for weeks. I thought I was a goner. I really did. It takes all my strength to get here today, but, well, after your poor ma, I had to come and see how you were diddlin'."

Mabel's eyes stung, and she didn't have the strength to reveal the pain in her heart. Besides, she didn't want to burden Lydia with her woes when it had been such a struggle to visit. So instead, the girl clamped her lips together, hoping that to outsiders, the expression resembled a smile.

"I'm sorry, Harry couldn't make it," she said, "but he does send his best wishes. I keep telling him he needs to get you that job he promised, get you out of here. But there's some sort of hold up. Big wigs wrangling about contracts, he reckons."

Relaxing a little, the inmate girl began to explain about the infirmary.

"Well, it sounds like you've fallen on your feet. So that's a plus, eh?"

As she continued, Mabel was distracted by Lydia's constant fidgeting as she searched through her bag.

"Harry told me to give you this."

Lydia snuck a boiled sweet into Mabel's hand. She popped the humbug into her mouth, and the minty sugary flavour flooded her senses. Exquisite! After months of bread, gruel, and the occasional watery soup, the taste was like heaven on earth.

All too soon, the handbell rang, marking the end of visiting time, and the women said their farewells.

As Mabel headed to the dining room for the evening meal, she walked past the chapel. Reverend Bennett was changing the numbers on the hymn board.

"Ah, Miss Nithercott. I'm glad I've seen you. Take this envelope, read the contents when you're back in the dormitory. I think you will find this information useful."

The reverend checked no one had witnessed the transaction then tapped the side of his nose.

"Let's keep this our little secret, Mabel."

In silence, Mabel forced down another bowl of the dismal gruel as her left hand stroked the envelope tucked in her waistband. Upstairs she changed into her nightdress. Once more, the mistress did her night-time inspections, berating anyone who fell short. Normally, the master and mistress were a married couple, but not here. That went some way to explaining why she was far less accommodating than the governor.

Once the dormitory door was locked, Mabel slipped under her covers and waited for everyone to settle, her ears on high alert. This was her chance. She balanced on her bedstead, hoping to catch the last of the evening moonlight to read by.

"Can't you be quiet?" grizzled a voice as the metal frame squeaked and groaned.

She teased out the envelope, slid her finger under the sealed flap, then opened it a quarter-inch at a time. The note was barely the size of her palm when she unfolded it, but it had the power to change her life forever.

London Metropolitan Board of Health

Having offered FOUR SCHOLAR-
SHIPS To enable Persons to
Receive Instruction in Nursing At
a Training Institution.

Candidates are requested to forward their names and all
particulars to
MISS GERTRUDE BARNARD-
ISTON, The Ryes, Sudbury,
Suffolk, who will give any information required. Candidates must
be respectable unmarried young
women between 16 and 25 years
of age. They will be employed by
the Suffolk Nursing Association after training.

Please apply by letter in the first
instance.

Her excitement was palpable. The question now was,
how could she apply for a bursary without a pen, paper, or any other means of communication with the
outside world? Perhaps Simeon could help her? If he
did, would it be in time to meet the looming deadline?

Little did she know, the limited availability of sta-
tionery was the least of her problems.

16

INJUSTICE

Although younger inmates benefited from Mr Emsworth's liberal approach to reformation, the local community was infuriated by his progressive ideas. The nearby industrialists, who bore the financial burden of caring for the workhouse inmates, were furious. Not only did they have to pay high taxes to fund parish contributions, but they also had to deal with a militant workforce that was becoming more unionised by the day, demanding better working conditions and fewer hours, all of which decimated their bottom line. They felt associations like the Guinness and Peabody Trust gave the working classes ideas beyond their station.

With each new workhouse initiative from Emsworth, the dissenting voices grew louder. The announcement of the Christian Women's Mission library donation had been the final straw. The guardians decided to take decisive action. In the lavish meeting room at Stepney Town Hall that evening, tempers frayed beyond repair. It was going to be an administrative witch hunt, and the committee was relishing the prospect of the kill.

The chairman, Solomon Caxton, spoke first.

"While we acknowledge that Mr Emsworth's public infirmary trial is a success and a significant source of revenue, we believe his practice of rewarding reforming inmates goes against how a workhouse should be run. Worse, encouraging outside intervention from charitable organisations such as Tynedale Hall and the mission has enabled the provision of care above and beyond the statutory minimum set by the government. Perks, if you will. We can all agree that it started innocently enough, with good intentions of used toys for orphans and the like, but quickly spiralled out of control. This wretched library is a case in point. Compared to other, harsher institutions in the country, St Olave's risks being perceived as a soft option. Is Mr Emsworth trying to market the place like a five-star hotel, with full occupancy every night? If that is the case, may I remind him of his remit!"

"Hear! Hear!" bayed the throng.

"The parish is expected to provide a basic level of support for those in dire need. Yet, it seems each week, another privilege is granted. Are we going to condone rewarding the lazy and indolent or rid the organisation of this weakness? And by weakness, I mean you, Mr Emsworth. Not only have you flagrantly bent the rules of the workhouse, but it seems you have been awarding positions of employment and lucrative contracts to your cronies."

As he listened to the blatant character assassination, Mr Emsworth's breathing became laboured and shallow.

"What do you have to say for yourself, man?"

"Like Thomas Barnardo and William Booth of the Salvation Army, I am an educated Christian man. Did the Lord not say to us, "Whoever is generous to the poor lends to the Lord, and he will repay him for his deed." Isn't it better for us to train our inmates to work hard for queen, country, and empire? Why should we not educate them, improve their literacy, numeracy, and manual dexterity so that they can go out to work for fine organisations that so many of you here own? Those who choose to study after finishing their workhouse duties will strive to be more diligent, effective, and productive workers. Sirs, that must be in both yours and their best interests?"

Some of the committee nodded, others scribbled notes ready to take the governor to task over his liberal comments.

"I fail to see how putting an inexperienced young lad to work on the kitchen allotment who then takes up a permanent gardening position outside St Olave's is a poor decision.

I have helped him escape the workhouse rather than be eternally trapped in it! You also want to keep people out of the workhouse. All we differ on is the method."

On hearing Mr Emsworth's contrarian attitude, Solomon Caxton almost snapped his pen.

"The Salvation Army has done fantastically well with their temperance movement, addressing the rabble in music halls, church halls and from makeshift podiums in parks. He has galvanised many a drunken labourer into action to reform their ways, turn their back on the demon drink, encourage them to provide for their families rather than boozing away their savings. Why should I not do the same thing? Why should I not lift deserving inmates out of the gutter?"

"It is quite simple, governor. The workhouse is a place of punishment, not development. You have been warned on several occasions that your work, and your partnership with Tynedale Hall, is undermining the purpose of the institution under your stewardship. We have no alternative but to relieve you of your position immediately."

"But," protested Emsworth, unable to be heard above the jubilant cheers.

Solomon banged his gavel, trying to hush the mob.

"You are to leave this town hall and return to your quarters in the workhouse, pack your belongings and vacate the premises. The porters, under the guidance of Mr McLaughlin, have been instructed to help you move to a new location."

"Where?"

"I suggest you find yourself a hotel for tonight. Perhaps your soft-touch side-kick, Reverend Bennett, will live up to his lofty ideals and put a roof over your head in the longer term?"

"This is unforgivable," protested the governor ."Under what authority can you remove me from my position? I do not recognise this gathering."

The chairman smirked at Mr McLaughlin.

"I'm afraid we can, and we are."

A door opened   at the back. A man entered the room, thin, wiry, and brusque. His sullen demeanour made Emsworth feel like a thundercloud had arrived instead.

"Ah, Mr Pickering. Excellent timing."

Mr Emsworth looked horrified.

"At least let me call on Reverend Bennett on the way to St Olave's. See if he has a bed for me?"

Caxton rolled his eyes, huffed, then nodded, unaware the real reason for his request was to forewarn Simeon of Pickering the Punisher's arrival.

*

After frowning at him, fate now smiled on Douglas. Simeon put Mr Emsworth up in one of the spare rooms allocated for the lecturer's lodgings. Soon, his possessions were bouncing along in his luggage trunks on the back of a cart heading for Tynedale Hall.

On Emsworth's arrival, the reverend was waiting on the steps with two strapping hall wardens.

"Men, can you take these crates to room twenty-six, please? I need to speak to Mr Emsworth alone."

The wardens heaved the crates off the wagon as the two friends marched to the reverend's quarters.

"They might be able to oust you, Douglas, but they cannot remove a representative of the Lord as easily. Frederick Temple, the Bishop of London, has appointed me to oversee St Olave's religious activities. And I will not neglect our flock."

Simeon poured out a large whiskey and offered it to his sorrowful friend.

"Please try and relax."

"Not much chance of that," Emsworth complained bitterly.

"That was an order, not a suggestion," countered Bennett. "I will continue to do my rounds, keep an eye on Miss Nithercott, and the others with a vocational placement. If Caxton and his chums want to make my life difficult, the Christian missionaries will be my eyes and ears. They cannot expel everyone from the workhouse who seeks to improve the lives of the deserving poor."

Alas, the reverend had underestimated the situation, his optimistic outlook misplaced.

"Anyway, who is the new appointee, Douglas? Who will be sticking their nose into our business?"

"Pickering, the former head of Andover."

"Andover! Good grief! Wasn't that the place where the rations were docked so often that the male inmates resorted to eating the rotting scraps of marrow from the old bones they were supposed to crush. Utterly barbaric that fellow, Pickering. He will make it difficult for us to provide assistance."

"He will make 'being difficult' his life's work," Douglas complained, nodding.

"We'll have to take it easy for a while, let things settle down, and then get back to work."

"Work? I have no idea what I will do next, Simeon. Another governorship will be out of the question. Once the papers report on my dismissal, that avenue will be closed off permanently. That scoundrel Caxton will want to shame me publicly, no doubt. I might contact Barnardo or Booth."

"We have another group of university undergraduates coming to stay with us before the Autumn term begins. Perhaps you can be their concierge? It will provide you with an income whilst you work out what you will do next. They do good work in the parish. Legal advice, engineering tuition, even one don who wants to teach Italian—."

"Buona fortuna to finding any takers with that around here!" chuckled Douglas, his mood lifting a little. "I can't thank you enough, Simeon. You are a fine man. I am sure you make the good Lord proud."

*

At that late hour, news of Mr Emsworth's dismissal had not yet reached the infirmary, thus Mabel was unaware that her nursing opportunity was about to be removed. Instead, the young woman was helping sister with Mr Harris. In the past month, there had been a marked decline in his mental faculties, making him increasingly difficult to care for. Despite his frail appearance, his temper had given him the strength of an ox.

"Get! Off! Me!"

Beresford dodged a punch, then grabbed Edward by the forearms.

"Get me another dressing!" roared sister as she fought to restrain the man. "Now!"

"Yes, of course," said Mabel, reluctant to leave her superior alone with the maniac.

She passed another gauze pad just as Harris's foot kicked out at her hand. The sterile dressing fell on the floor for a split second. Mabel swooped to retrieve it.

"Heavens, girl, have you learned nothing! Are you trying to give him septicaemia? Get a fresh piece. Quickly!"

The snarled criticism stung. The chastised girl scurried off to the storeroom, hunting for a big carton of gauze. Things were still in a bit of a mess in there after the collapse of the storage unit a few days ago. Where could it be? Her search was interrupted when she heard her name called, not by sister, but by Mrs Fishwick.

"Mabel! Come now!" shrieked the old woman.

She spied Mr Harris was out of bed, delirious and agitated. He had Sister Beresford in a headlock, attempting to wring her neck like a Christmas goose. The girl instinctively ran to her aid. As the brute tightened his grip, Beresford's eyes bulged like a toad's and her face became flushed. Edward babbled uncontrollably. It was like he was speaking a foreign language, or possessed perhaps. Mabel tried to prise him off Beresford, but he was too strong.

"Do something!" squawked Mrs Fishwick.

Mabel returned to the storeroom, grabbed a bottle of chloroform, and poured some onto a cotton pad. The pungent chemical dripped off the dressing as she hurried back. Putting the rag over Harris's nose and mouth, within seconds, he was incapacitated. He fell back heavily towards the bed, dragging sister with him. As his grip loosened on her windpipe, Beresford collapsed on the floor like a felled tree. Mabel slapped her on the cheek and shook her violently.

"Sister Beresford! Wake up! Wake--up--!"

As the oxygen reached her brain once more, the groggy woman began to come around. Checking Edward was out for the count, Mabel escorted her to the nurse's desk. Then she got some crepe bandages and tied Mr Harris's wrists to his iron bedstead.

"Well done, Mabel," cheered Mrs Fishwick.
"That was a lucky escape."

Feeling a little better, Beresford marched to the double doors and bellowed for Mr McLaughlin's immediate assistance.

"Sister?" he beckoned.

"Get Harris in solitary confinement. Make sure you restrain him. I shall arrange his transfer in the morning," bellowed Beresford. "It's the asylum for him--we can't look after him here anymore."

McLaughlin organised two inmate wardens to drag Harris, still dead to the world, down to solitary confinement. When she first met Edward, Mabel thought back to what a jolly and kind-spirited patient he had been as she did that first bed change. But, alas, senility had robbed him of his good character and turned him into a violent monster.

In all the furore, there was a glimmer of opportunity for the girl. Sneaking a pen and paper out of the desk, Mabel decided to forget the attack by finally drafting her application for the bursary.

*

Relaxing after their successful coup, Soloman met Pickering in a private gentleman's club in Soho. Caxton puffed at a thick Cuban cigar as the new governor clicked his fingers and demanded another bottle of champagne.

"Finally, it's time for you to make a mark on St Olave's, Pickering."

"Indeed, it is," he replied. "It's time to show those wretched inmates who's the boss of the workhouse now."

*

At breakfast, Mr Pickering swooped into the workhouse dining room, his black frock coat flapping behind him as if the Grim Reaper himself had arrived. The first thing he did was break the rule of silence.

"As you may be aware, Mr Emsworth has been dismissed from St Olave's. I am Pickering, former governor of Andover, his replacement."

Worried glances were exchanged amongst the diners.

"The mistress and I will be in charge now. The guardians are determined that the workhouse reverts to its more traditional footing, providing beds and food in exchange for hard labour. Only male orphans under the age of fifteen will be given vocational instruction. Those of you who have been working in the kitchen garden or the infirmary will be assigned new jobs as cleaners, cooks, or laundresses, as I see fit. There will be no reading visits from the mission on Sundays."

Mabel's stomach clenched. If only she had secured that nursing apprenticeship. Despite months of loyal service, she was being forcibly removed from the infirmary. Coming from a poor background, reverting to basic duties in the workhouse would surely jeopardise her application?

As Emsworth's flagship pet project, Pickering cheerfully reassigned her to the laundry to wash hundreds of heavily soiled bed sheets. The time dragged. Since the death of her mother, she'd felt lonelier than ever. Now she didn't have the companionship of Peggy or Ada, nor the guidance of Sister Beresford, or Mr Emsworth, she felt even more rudderless. Simeon was also conspicuous in his absence. She longed for Lydia's next visit. It was her only hope to smuggle out her crusade to join the Twining Institute for Nursing. Finally, McLaughlin came to see her in the laundry with some good news, uttering the words nearly choked him.

"Nithercott! Visitors. Now."

At the far side of the public parlour room sat Lydia looking a little bit perkier, with Harry alongside her.

"Mabel, dear! How are you? What's all this about Mr Emsworth running off to Tynedale Hall! It's the talk of the street? All a bit sudden, wasn't it? Milly said something about corruption?"

"I sincerely doubt that. This place is run like a cabal now--everything is for the guardians' benefit. Only the orphans get any help. We get to hear about our shifts, and everything else about this place seems to be top secret."

"There's been no news of your father," said Harry." However, he might be due out soon for good behaviour--if he managed to control that temper of his."

Mabel didn't really care what her father was up to anymore. The only thing that mattered was following her vocation--nursing--which had suffered a significant setback without Emsworth's patronage.

The warm summer sun burst through the visitor room window and the heat made Lydia drowsy. She began to nod off in the chair, her head sinking forward until her chin almost touched her chest, then snapping back on autopilot.

"How is she doing?" whispered Mabel. "She looks healthy enough but tired."

"She's coping," Harry confirmed. "But she's not as bossy as she used to be, though. All that time sat down because of the pneumonia, well, it knocked the stuffing out of her. She won't go to the market on her own anymore. Milly Compton goes if she needs anything urgently and I'm not there. She's not too steady on her feet."

He deftly sidestepped the depressing topic.

"The good news is, it looks like the job at the exchange is back on. We should be fitting the desks out next week. Within six weeks, the telephone network should be fully operational, and then they'll be hiring the telephonists. You'll be brilliant at it. And, better still, I'm sure you'll have enough money to treat me to a night at the music hall and a slap-up meal to say thank you?"

Mabel caught her breath as he gave her his customary roguish wink.

"I love a bit of music, don't you? A good sing-along with a nice pint of mild helps me unwind. We've had a few good nights at the Drummer Boy these past few weeks. Fergus has put on some fantastic acts and a couple of bare-knuckle fights upstairs, on the quiet."

"These days, Prospect Street seems like a different lifetime."

"Keep your chin up. You'll be out soon."

"In the meantime, Harry, I was wondering if you could smuggle something out for me."

"Course! You know me. I like a bit of duckin' and divin'. What is it? Baccy, you won playing a midnight game of cards?"

"Stop being ridiculous. This is important."

"So, what is it then?"

"Nothing much, just an envelope. Can you pop it in at the post office tomorrow?"

"All right. Yer on," whispered Harry.

After making sure no one was looking, he put his cloth cap on the table, and Mabel slid the correspondence underneath it.

"Can't be too careful, H. I don't trust anyone here now, except for Sister Beresford, and I don't see her anymore."

He let his calloused fingers rub along the back of her soft hand. She blushed. That tingle was there again. Visiting time was nearly over, and Mabel gently shook Lydia by the shoulder.

"Come on, now. Wakey, wakey, my lovely. You've got to get Harry back home."

Dazed and dozy, Lydia pushed hard off the arms of the winged chair and eventually got to her feet.

"Now, you go steady. Look after her, Harry, won't you?"

"Yes, Mabel, of course. Anything for my dear old Ma."

"And you won't forget, the--er--" she said, miming the outline of the envelope.

"You can rely on me. Nothing to worry about on that score," he said, carefully putting the cap in his blazer pocket, concealing the note perfectly.

As Harry took his mother by the arm and led her to the exit. Mabel returned to the laundry for one more hour of backbreaking work, followed by watery soup. Harry escorted his mother back home, making sure she didn't trip over the cobbles. It took longer to get back than he'd hoped. Finally, he toppled her into her rocking chair and made his excuse to leave.

"I'm parched ma, time for a pint over the road. Be a treasure, and keep my dinner warm. Not sure when I'll be back. Bye!"

The door slammed shut, and Mrs Kirkham was alone again.

Harry arrived just in time to see the first round of an underground bare-knuckle fight Jimmy McGinty had put on. He had two shillings on one of the bruisers to win and was keen to cheer him along from the ropes. Two pints followed in quick succession. Even more of his wages were gambled on the second match. Harry was thoroughly immersed in the bout.

"Give him a good wallop. Yeah! Another one of them hooks!"

Craving a smoke, he put his hand in his pocket and took out his cigarette-rolling machine. As he pulled out the metal contraption, Mabel's precious application fluttered to the floor, the envelope soon trodden into the wet floorboards by dozens of hobnail boots. Thus, Harry's boozy oversight would herald the end of Mabel's nursing career through no fault of her own.

Stuck in St Olave's, poor Mabel knew nothing about it.

17

RULE OF THE TYRANT

Back at the infirmary, Pickering had been forced to eat his words, and worse, relent in his reign of tyranny. He wanted to keep the committee sweet and continue his brutal cutting of corners. But equally, he needed to keep the inspectors, and medical officers satisfied that a reasonable standard of care was provided. After the cruelty in Andover, he would be a figure of suspicion.

The past few weeks had seen a wave of disease sweep through London and the workhouse, taking down the sick, old, and infirm like a scythe through a field of wheat. Only the strongest inmates were able to survive, and that was down to the care provided by Sister Beresford and her team of trainees. She was livid that she kept receiving the imbeciles the other workhouse departments refused, especially after the baby-scalding near-miss earlier in the year.

After the last inspection, the committee had received complaints from the medical officer that the standard of care had deteriorated because of the 'reliance on imbecile staff'. Mr Pickering had no option but to reinstate Mabel. The decision riled him; she was one of Tynedale Hall's philanthropic poster girls. He decided it was better to swallow his pride than to provoke the wrath of the inspectors. Increased inspections, especially flying visits, severely curtailed his ability to inflict his cruel whims on the inmates.

*

Archie had struggled with the agonising wait. It had been an eternity since he had last seen Mabel, and with the regime change, he was concerned about her. He wanted to ask Sister Beresford about her whereabouts more than anything else but felt it was inappropriate.

It took a while for one of his deliveries and Mabel's shift to coincide. Stretched and exhausted, the ward sister had preferred to put Mabel on night duty so that she could get some proper rest. Caring for such a high volume of patients with inmate staff who had no talent for healthcare had been frustrating. She was relieved when Mr Pickering had relented and let Mabel resume her post. It was like being thrown a lifeline.

As time dragged on, Mabel felt more despondent about the scholarship. She had decided Louisa Twining was not as egalitarian as she implied in her adverts. Reverend Simeon had heard nothing either, and the deadline for applications had long since passed.

Archie had started piling extra items onto his sack trolley, hoping that Mabel would get to hold the door open for him or assist with unloading, engineering the perfect cover story to talk to her. The longer things went on, the more determined he became to strike up a conversation. Day after day, he pulled up his cart in the workhouse delivery area and stacked the trolley up to the handles. He would enter the in-mate wing, pushing his back against the double doors, fighting to get the trolley through the gap. He huffed, puffed, groaned, and stopped every couple of yards to reposition the stock in an attempt to extend the length of his visit.

At last, he looked around and saw Mabel talking to Mrs Fishwick.

"Could you help me?" he mouthed.

Mabel nodded and excused herself to her patient.

"You look troubled, Archie."

His face fell further.

"What's wrong?"

"It's my mother. A week ago, she left unex-pectedly on an urgent errand. My Aunt Nelly, her youngest sister, is gravely ill. Her doctor gave her only three months to live. She has six children under the age of ten. As you might imagine, my mother's unexpected de-parture has left a void in our household. My father and I aren't very good at looking after ourselves. We have no friends or family to turn to. Life is difficult because of the long hours we work."

Archie broke off the conversation to peer out the storeroom, concerned that her absence would be noticed. Sister Beresford was elsewhere, so he continued.

"Because we're so busy, my father and I don't have time to interview someone from an agency."

"I'm confused—"

"I know it would be a huge sacrifice for you to leave the infirmary for good, but we desperately need help. I was thinking, if you could assist my father in the pharmacy in the long run, the suggestion may be appealing? We can provide you with bed and board, of course, and perhaps some extra money for your troubles. That's if you want to help us."

Mabel's heart was torn. If only she'd heard about her application, the decision would have been much easier.

"I'm so sorry, Archie, but I can't risk it. Girls from Prospect Street never rise to the top. They only sink to the bottom. Unless I am blessed with a miracle, I have to pin my hopes on that bursary."

"But what happens when this wave of sickness passes? Mr Pickering will most likely send you back to the laundry. Is that what you want?"

Mabel felt in an impossible situation. If she was honest, she was starting to give up hope of ever getting the scholarship. The longer she waited for a response from the foundation, the more demoralised she became. The ogre Pickering was determined to eliminate all workhouse rewards, no matter how small. She thought back to the day when she arrived and looked at the grey washerwomen. How would she get a message to Archie? What if she changed her mind? She nearly said yes to him there and then but bit her tongue. Hold on a little longer, she told herself. Better safe than sorry.

"Are you still listening to me, Mabel?"

"Forgive me. Yes. You've taken me by surprise, but I shall consider your offer. I promise. When are you due here with your next delivery?"

"Tuesday. Late in the afternoon. Last drop off."

"Miss Nithercott!"

Mabel jumped a mile. Sister Beresford was stood brooding at the doorway.

"Am I interrupting your little tete-a-tete? Have you forgotten your responsibility to the patients?"

"No, sister," she replied, mortified.

Archie finished unloading the stock and left, utterly disappointed that he had not convinced her there and then. She hoped that when it came time for her to return to the laundry, Sister Beresford would be strong enough to stand up to Mr Pickering. But sadly, when the matter came to a head, sister was roundly defeated.

"Mabel's placement must come to an end, or we will have a rebellion on our hands with the committee members."

"I want her out of here by Sunday. The guardians have said that favouritism will not be tolerated. You will have to make do with whatever inmates are allocated to you. Is that understood?"

Sister Beresford's eyes narrowed with hatred before she begrudgingly agreed.

Mabel's thoughts were completely consumed by Archie's offer as she lay in bed that night. She put the scholarship idea aside for a moment and let her mind fill with bigger, bolder, and brighter images. One of her favourite pastimes in the grey, prison-like work-house was fantasising about the outside world. She remembered the music halls, the colourful parks with bandstands, the lidos, strolling by the Thames. Then the dark clouds reappeared. The oppressive regime within the workhouse, particularly in the laundry. She had to make a choice! It might be rewarding at the pharmacy, she mused. She lay back on her straw mattress, staring up at the ceiling, her mind flipping through her options. She was tired of being paralysed, tired of relying on other people, tired of having no control over her future, tired of being at the mercy of other people's whims.

The next morning the harpy of a mistress came around for her usual, terse inspection of their room.

"Nithercott, come here."

Mabel wondered what she'd done wrong. Her bed looked immaculate, hospital corners and all.

"Today, you will be allocated to a new area. The laundry. Your assistance is no longer required in the infirmary."

Mabel opened her mouth to protest, but the mistress carried on like a steamroller.

"--The matter has been resolved with Sister Beresford. Please report to the laundry after breakfast."

Mabel tried to work out what day it was, counting them on her fingers. Oh no! Tuesday!

It took barely an hour in the laundry to convince Mabel that Archie's offer was her only hope. The question was, how to get in touch with him? She was certain that any written attempt to send a message would be thwarted by Mr Pickering. He seemed to relish inflicting suffering, delighting in making an example of her to the other inmates.

Archie arrived in the ward, but Mabel was nowhere to be seen.

"Do you need a hand," asked Sister Beresford, holding the swing doors open for him.

"If you wouldn't mind, thank you. Er, I can't see Miss Nithercott. She's not come down with this terrible bug, has she?"

"No, she bides fine. Well, as fine as can be expected, now she's been relegated to laundry work."

He went into a panic. How could he sneak her out now he didn't know where she was? Then, on his way back to the delivery yard, he noticed another store cupboard, this time housing the wardens' uniforms. That's it, he thought.

He took an outfit off the rack and put it on, then hid another in one of his delivery boxes. Peering through the tiny storeroom window, he noticed the female yard. The washerwomen were making trips back and forth with the clean linen. He tried to make sense of his unfamiliar surroundings and guessed that if he took the corridor to the left, he would be heading in the right direction.

Like a deadly assassin, he crept along the passageway until he found himself staring into the female courtyard. There was no sign of Mabel. He waited. Every second felt like a year. Then he noticed a forlorn-looking figure with her head bowed and shoulders rounded. Her whole body language suggested a person who was oppressed and depressed. Near the end of her shift, drudgery had devoured all her joy.

Through some sort of Kismet, their eyes met across the yard. Just a few hours working as a workhouse washerwoman had given Mabel the answer she was looking for. Escaping with Archie was the best thing she could do.

Silently, Archie motioned for Mabel to come over, his gesture clear.

"Quick, we haven't got much time!"

Keeping a keen eye out for the menace that was Mr McLaughlin, they sneaked into the corridor.

"How will you get me out? It's a dead cert I'll be captured in this uniform."

"With this--"

Archie flipped the uppermost box open, revealing the warden's uniform.

Mabel smiled.

"This way," she said, nodding her head in the direction of the inspection room from her first night.

The awful tin bath was still in the middle, minus the dingy, cold water. Carefully, she closed the door.

"You listen out for footsteps while I put this on."

Archie pressed his ear to the door as she whipped off her inmate uniform and slid into the warden's one. Then tucked her hair into the cap and pulled the brim down as low as it would go to complete the disguise.

"I'm ready. Let's go!" she murmured.

The two of them wheeled the trolley together, pretending the load was a heavy two-man job.

Mabel was desperate to run as he led her to the delivery bays, but she knew it would draw too much attention. Finally, as they opened the door to the open courtyard, the young woman had never felt such a joyous sense of freedom simply from staring at the dark grey skyline of Whitechapel!

"Meet Toby," Archie said, patting the beast on the neck while keeping his eyes peeled for unwanted observers. "Quick. Get under here."

He drew a tarpaulin to one side of the cart and made a step for her by bending down and interlocking his fingers. She scurried beneath the rough fabric. They both stifled a laugh as he covered her up. Then, Archie hopped into the driver's seat and yanked on the reins of the lovely chestnut horse.

"Gee up, Toby. We've got work to do. This important delivery won't get there itself."

He turned the cart round. In the darkness, Mabel listened to the rhythmic clip-clop of Toby's hooves. Minutes later, peering from under the tarp, she knew she was free for the first time in months as they sped off together to Blackheath.

When it was safe, Archie pulled up, and she joined him on the driver's seat.

I can't believe I'm doing this!" Mabel confessed with a smile.

"I promise you it will be worth it. You're one of a kind, Mabel, and I'll take good care of you."

Her cheeks flushed. She turned to look away into the street.

"It's a long time since I've seen any of this," she said, changing the subject.

Recognising one or two of the sellers her parents used to talk to in the Drummer Boy, she pulled down the brim of her cap. The last thing she wanted was her father knowing that she had escaped the work-house. He would expect her to become his skivvy again.

Archie guided Toby through the archway to the left of his father's pharmacy and tethered him up in the backyard.

"I suppose you better meet my father then."

The brass doorbell chimed as Archie pushed open the entrance. A middle-aged man was behind the counter, gently rolling a bar of pliable white matter on a special tray, lowering down a wire mesh, much like a cheesemonger would. Rows of neatly formed little pills appeared. Concentrating so hard, the chemist hadn't noticed the doorbell.

"Father."

"What's going on? Who's this?" Charles de-manded, noticing his son had appeared with a woman dressed in men's clothing.

Mabel hoped the confusion was due to her attire.

"I've taken matters into my own hands, fa-ther. This is Miss Nithercott, Mabel Nithercott."

"Ye gods! Why's she dressed like a man? Have you brought a lunatic home?"

Archie sidestepped the question.

"I met her in the workhouse infirmary caring for the inmates. I thought she could help us. She is honest, diligent and hardworking."

"Honest? The girl is wearing a cloth cap and trousers!"

"She's also studied Honnor Morton's nursing books. So, she can help us in the pharmacy if it gets hectic. And she'll be able to help us with the housework for a month or two until mother gets back."

From the tone of the conversation, it was clear to Mabel that Archie had never broached the subject of her appointment with his father until now.

"Have you gone mad? Smuggling a girl from the workhouse? It's preposterous. Well, you can jolly well take her back--this instant!"

"Father, please! We can't cope without mother. Not with our workload. We have no clean clothes. We've barely eaten a proper meal in days."

"Fiddlesticks!"

"It's true! Grabbing a few hours' sleep and working every minute God sends? We cannot carry on like this. We need help, so Miss Nithercott is staying."

The two men stared at each other like rabid wolves, waiting for the other one to make the first move.

"All right. But only on a trial basis."

Mabel was crushed by Archie's deception. She scowled at him, kicking herself for being so stupid as to destroy her slim nursing prospects in favour of this farce.

"Where's she going to sleep, Archie? You tell me? We only have two bedrooms above the shop. Yours--and mine."

"Already dealt with, father. I've arranged for a mattress to be delivered later this evening. It can go in the back."

"--In my office, you mean!"

"Yes. Out of the way, under the stairs."

Under the stairs? Mabel felt she'd been reduced to nothing more than a common guard dog!

"Father, I'm sure Miss Nithercott will be able to find lodgings above one of the local shops once we've settled into our new routine. This will do for now. Many shopkeepers on the High Street don't live above their businesses and will appreciate having a reliable long-term tenant. This sleeping arrangement is an interim measure to resolve our immediate problem."

Charles muttered to himself as he slid the pills he'd made into a dark brown bottle. The Nithercott sur-name sounded horribly familiar, but he couldn't fathom why. Mabel decided that being polite was the best way to handle the fraught situation. She needed to build a bridge with Archie's father, and quickly. She took her cap off, letting her hair tumble down, and then did the best thing she could think of--lying earnestly and straight to his face.

"I'm looking forward to assisting you, Mr Stanford, whether at home or in the shop. I am confident that I will adjust quickly and be an asset to you."

Being a glorified charwoman was the last thing she wanted. She yearned to apply for more scholarships. At the least, sending the letters off would be easier now Mr Pickering's censorship of communications was no longer an issue.

Still bristling with rage, Charles was thudding and banging about as he worked. Irritated by his father's childish display of stubbornness, Archie left him to it and went to feed Toby. Mr Stanford abandoned any attempt at courtesy when he and Mabel were alone.

"Why don't you get yourself to work, Miss Nithercott. Start earning your keep?" snapped Mr Stanford. "The range needs at-tention. I suggest you start there. You'll find a tin of black lead and some wire wool in the cupboard. I expect it to be sparklingly clean by the end of the day."

"Yes, of course, Mr Stanford. As you wish."
Mabel replied through gritted teeth.

"And get out of that ridiculous outfit before
any of my customers see you."

Mabel sniffed dismissively. How could she meet that
request with only the clothes she was standing in to
her name? She headed to the back door to seek
Archie's advice. To the rear of the back office, she
spied a brown paper parcel on the table. On closer
inspection, it had her name on it. After undoing the
wrapping paper, she spied a second-hand housemaid's uniform, accompanied with a note.

"I hope this fits and that you will be happy
here."

Mabel had no idea if either of his hopes would happen. She hurried to the outside privy and got
changed, furious with Archie, even if he had acted out
of the best of intentions.

The maid's uniform looked nothing like a nurses. She hated
it instantly. It reeked of 'skivvy' not 'skilled'.

18

FROSTY RECEPTION

Once changed into her servant garb, Mabel rolled up her sleeves and set to work. The cooker was in an appalling condition. Where it wasn't encrusted with fat, it was covered in rust. She rummaged around in the cupboard and took out the tin of Zebra Range and Grate Blacking. She dabbed some steel wool in the tin and then rubbed with all her might to restore the device to its former glory. Her progress was even slower than when she had cleaned the windows at Prospect Street. Still, there was no use complaining about it. The only way to impress Charles Stanford would be through sheer elbow grease. Dismayed, she felt that after two hours, it was impossible to tell if anything had changed, apart from the cuffs on her uniform had started to take on the same blackness as the grubby metal.

Aching all over, she took a breather and shook her forearms to loosen the muscles. On the mantelpiece was a photograph of Archie, Charles, and his wife. Mabel thought she looked a kindly sort and wondered if she might get to meet the woman one day.

Downstairs, Archie, and Charles were beavering away to get the orders ready for the next day's deliveries.

"I am dreading the end of the workhouse contract," complained Charles. "I got complacent, foolish. I should have drummed up more business elsewhere. We're going to feel the pinch without it. St Olave's was our biggest customer."

"We'll be alright, father. We'll think of something. We always do."

"We've got enough savings to pay for the rent for another three months, and then, Archie, well, I just don't know."

"Tell you what, leave these last bits to me. You can rearrange the window display, make it a bit more eye-catching? Why don't you put some of that gripe water out? We have boxes of it in the back, and new mothers constantly ask for it."

"Yes, that's a good idea, son. Although they're so cheap, we'll have to sell hundreds of those a week to stay afloat," he muttered. "Can't see that happening!"

"What was that, father? You weren't moaning again, were you?" Archie questioned.

"Me? Moaning? Whatever do you mean? You sound like your mother," he chuckled, as for

once, the Old curmudgeon looked on the
bright side.

Mr Stanford's woes were understandable. Their
commercial contracts were dwindling, and retail
sales were slowing too. But, much to Charles's cha-
grin, everyone seemed to be buying Cornelius
Quimby's new miracle cure. Nevertheless, he remained unconvinced about its efficacy. How could it
possibly work? With no formal pharmaceutical
training, he thought Quimby was nothing more than
a charlatan.

Just like Mabel, Charles had also noticed Quimby's
embrocation adverts in the paper. Recently, it
seemed that not only was Cornelius advertising his
wares directly to customers, but he was also recruit-
ing what amounted to a small army of travelling
salesmen to join his enterprise, tasked with fulfilling
orders to pharmacies and cottage hospitals up and
down the land. Worse, his garishly packaged products seemed to be taking over the whole world.
Charles had taken an interest in his punishing itiner-
ary, the odious man's tours to Ireland and Scotland,
North America, and Africa, creating hysteria wherever he went.

> "If only I had the wherewithal to produce a
> product to compete with him," mused
> Charles as he finished his display of gripe
> water.

He admired his handiwork, the neat rows of bottles standing perfectly aligned on his stepped shelves. Mabel tiptoed downstairs, not wanting to interrupt the men as they beavered away, but they still heard her.

"I just came to tell you dinner's ready. I'll keep it simmering on the hob until you're ready."

The meal was nothing special, but she hoped it would be filling. She had created a simple soup of bread, onions, milk and water. The larder was almost bare without Mrs Stanford's wifely touch to keep it well stocked. There wasn't even a tin of cheap corned beef. Worried the meal would be bland, she gave the thick mixture a little grating of nutmeg, and a generous pinch of salt, hoping that that would be enough to add a little interest. She had no idea what she was going to make the next day. The two men came upstairs.

"I'll leave you alone," she said.

"Don't be silly. Stay with us," reassured Archie.

As Charles kicked his son hard in the shin, Mabel heard the scrape of a sole on the floorboards. The three of them sat in silence, the atmosphere tense.

"The bits of the range you worked on this afternoon look like new, Mabel. What do you say, father?"

Charles, jabbing at his meal rather than eating it, simply grunted incoherently. The awkwardness was punctuated by a knock at the door. Archie ran down to greet the caller. Finally finishing his food, Charles lumbered across to his favourite seat, an armchair facing the window onto Blackheath Common. Mabel cleared away the pots.

Downstairs, she heard Archie thanking someone, then a dragging sound. It seemed her new mattress had been delivered. The young man tucked it under the stairs, out of sight. He was delighted. It fitted perfectly. Better still, it was completely out of view from anyone standing in the shop. Tongues wagging about the strange girl staying while his mother was away was something he wanted to avoid. If asked, he would come clean and say Mabel was their new maid whilst his mother was indisposed with the family matter. For now, he hoped that her residency would remain secret, for a day or two at least, so that Charles had time to warm to her before the busy bodies came into the shop to find out for themselves.

The young fellow trotted upstairs. Seeing his father dozing in the chair, his full belly making him drowsy, Archie motioned for Mabel to come and look at her meagre 'sleeping quarters'. Expecting something rough and ready, she was pleasantly surprised by his thoughtful addition of a plump pillow and a soft blanket.

"I'll see if I can get a bedframe. Raise it up a bit. It'll give you a place to store your things."

"I don't think I've got money for 'things', Archie," Mabel chuckled. "All I've got to my name is a workhouse warden's uniform. Given that it's obviously stolen, I don't think I'll bother taking it to the pawn shop."

She ran her hand along her new bed to check how comfortable it was. The mattress was made from the same striped fabric as the workhouse, but it had been stuffed with softer horsehair instead of straw, and it was completely free of those awful, gut-wrenching stains she had grown used to.

"Comfy?" Archie asked with a concerned tone.

"I shall sleep like a log. It will be a delight not to hear fellow inmates moaning and groaning at all hours, the wretched handbell clanging like clockwork, and the ominous footsteps of Mr McLaughlin on the prowl."

"Why don't you go upstairs and talk to your Pa? He seemed a bit surprised to see me," she said, raising her eyebrows, hoping to drag the truth out of her new companion.

"I may have glossed over a few details," Archie admitted. "But the thought of you locked in the workhouse weighed heavily on my mind, especially with Mr Pickering's appointment. Things were only going to get worse, and they weren't idyllic to start with. Admit it."

"Will you please stop fussing, Alastair? You're like a mother hen looking after her first brood of chicks. Prospect Street women can look after themselves as soon as the midwife cuts the cord."

Archie smiled as he got a small oil lamp for her.

"Am I allowed to give you this? Or would you prefer to set it up yourself?"

"Now you're being silly?" she said, grabbing the lamp from him with a smile. "Go and check if your father has calmed down."

"Probably not. He can be a real stick in the mud when he wants to be. He drives my mother round the bend at times," Archie said with a grin, "but she still loves him. He'll be alright. He just needs a bit of time. Once he's seen you are so much more than a plain old housemaid and will be an asset to the pharmacy, I'm sure he will ease up on you."

Mabel struck a match, the soft glow highlighting her pretty features.

"Night then."

"Night. And, er, thanks."

Despite Archie arranging a bed fit for a princess, Mabel lay wide awake, pondering her future. The question of whether the Twining's foundation had responded—or not—remained unanswered. How would she return to Tynedale Hall and the reverend to find out if she was at the Stanfords' beck and call all day long?

Upstairs, Charles had woken from his slumbers and treated himself to a little nose through the newspaper. A three-column feature on Quimby caught his eye.

"The Great Healer Rolls Into Gravesend."

It was a glowing piece revealing Cornelius, ever the showman was on a tour of Britain, and his next stop would be Blackheath.

"Right on my bloody doorstep," grizzled Charles, under his breath.

"Father? Is everything alright? Please tell me you're not still fretting about Mabel?"

"It's not that, son," he said, jabbing his finger at the article, "It's this. Look. The man could sell ice to Eskimos."

"Not Quimby again?" Archie said, picking up the paper.

He read the article, then looked at his father, his eyes twinkling.

"Instead of quibbling about him, Pa, why don't we order some of his products? Do some tests? See what's in these lotions and potions of his?"

"I doubt for a second there's anything of real medicinal value in there, Alastair. It's a-- what's the word?"

"Disaster—?"

"No, a placebo! It must be. How could a pil- lock like Quimby come up with anything of genuine medicinal value?"

The article featured some engraved sketches of 'Quimby the Showman' rolling into town with his brightly painted spectacle, causing quite a commo- tion.

"Listen to this," said Charles, flapping the pa- per loudly as he prepared to read.

"Quimby, the famous medicine man who has already created a considerable stir in the county of Kent, by the remarkable skills he possesses, has commenced operations in Gravesend.

A representative of this paper was able to get an op- portunity to speak privately with our distinguished visitor at Waterloo Place and had a very enjoyable time chatting with him. Quimby stated that he was in town to bring public awareness to his remedies and to appoint agents who could provide him with his oils and medicines in the future.

He spoke of his years on safari, stating that Africans believed anyone who had a toothache was under the control of an evil spirit, and there was no remedy for it. They thought he was supernatural because when he began to extract their aching teeth, then applied his soothing balm, the pain was gone for good.

Quimby soon became popular amongst the people. African doctors shared their methods with him. Because he has a natural flair for creating new treatments, they revered him, calling him 'mtu wa dawa,' or 'medicine man.'

He says European countries are ignorant of his remedies' potency.

The oily nature of the balm, for example, allows it to penetrate the skin, but only if applied properly. He added that the patient's blood must be purified using natural and safe internal medicine, such as his tincture, to fully heal. With repeated practice over two decades, Quimby says he has achieved proficiency in rubbing in twenty minutes, the same as an untrained person would do in an hour.

Although unconscious, patients occasionally winced during the rubbing. Once the procedure was finished, they regained consciousness almost immediately. Their faces radiated gratitude, and their tongues proclaimed to the crowd: 'All the pain is gone now.' The independent adjudicators, observers trained in Western medicine were astounded and overjoyed to have witnessed (first-hand) the curious man's ability to alleviate suffering.

Quimby is quick to point out to the public that he is not a 'doctor' or a 'quack.' Rather, he attempts to assist doctors and their currently imperfect medical science. Scam stories have reported that Quimby's Donegal estate is fenced with crutches taken from rheumatoid patients and paved with human teeth. He says he has met numerous people who refer to him as a trickster, a magician, a sorcerer, and a mesmerist, but he says 'it is like water off a duck's back.'

A significant fact in Quimby's favour is that these remedies have been used by over half a million people in the United Kingdom and Ireland, with astounding results.

Moreover, his wizardry is not limited to dentistry. In Poole, men who had not stood upright for years were now strong and capable of going to work, with no out-of-pocket expenses because he did all the work on his carriage for free. Quimby says he likes to promote his products with 'walking adverts.'

> Next week, Quimby will take his roadshow to
> Blackheath, South West London."

Charles looked at his son, the seed of a plan germinating in his crafty brain.

—

"There's our answer, Archie."

"We need to buy some of Quimby's products and test them?"

"No, Archibald, no! We need to go to the roadshow and see for ourselves! When Quimby rolls into Blackheath--we will be waiting for him!"

Archie worried about what his father meant as the two men retired to their beds.

It was getting late. Noticing her new master's bedroom door was open, Mabel went to check on him, thinking a hot drink might help him sleep. She crept upstairs and saw Charles reading the paper, still brooding over his plan to bring Quimby down a peg or two. She knocked gently.

"A cup of cocoa before bed, Mr Stanford?"

The interruption derailed his train of thought, and it annoyed him.

"Dear Lord, No. Get out, now. How dare you sneak up on me when I am in my own bed! Have you no manners, girl?"

Their frosty relationship continued in the same vein for several days. Finally, Archie tried to put Mabel's mind at rest, saying Charles was pining for his wife. He also mentioned there were money troubles with the sizable workhouse contract ending soon.

"It's not you. He's just a bit worn out with it all."

Mabel remained unconvinced.

"Perhaps you can find a way to warm his heart through his stomach?" joked Archie.

"I doubt that!"

"I have tried to persuade him, Mabel, but he's very stubborn when he wants to be. Just give it time. Hopefully, he'll get another work-house contract?"

"What's his favourite meal? Your father?"

"He likes colcannon."

"Right, I shall finish the laundry and then get the ingredients for it. The sooner I can start winning him over, the better," she said, taking a few coins from the petty cash tin.

A thought had been troubling Mabel for some time now, and she decided to share her concerns.

"Why doesn't your father offer mail-order medicines? I see Quimby has an advert on the front page most days. The strategy must work?"

"Like gangbusters, Mabel! But he's too stubborn to try!"

"Well, I think he should."

The evening meal had all the hallmarks of being a modest success. Mabel served hearty portions of hot buttery colcannon. The men began tucking into it. She left them alone.

"This is tasty, Pa, isn't it?"

"Passable. Not as good as your mother's, of course."

Archie sniffed in a long lungful of air.

"Mabel had an idea earlier. I think it has merit. It's err—mail order."

The suggestion was met with silence.

"I think you should at least consider it? When the shop is quiet, you have plenty of opportunities to make some of your signature pills. Especially with the death knell of the workhouse contract."

"You've not thought this through, have you, Archie? Unlike that quack Quimby, I use premium ingredients for my tablets, not the eyes of newts and toes of frogs and the like. You understand money is tight for us now. I can't afford the raw materials to even start. And the thought of standing at the counter rolling out more and more pills by hand, well, that's not something I relish the prospect of."

"There is another option," Archie pressed.

"What?"

"The work that Mabel was doing in the infirmary showed she had a real gift for treating wounds. She experimented with a poultice that treated bedsores, cuts, grazes, burns. She had success with the inmate trials and with her own brother. And, better still, because her family and Mr Emsworth were on such a tight budget—it's very reasonable to make."

"But you read the court case in the papers, Archie. William Nithercott died! It seems more of a poison than a potion. Those journalists will slay us. Her name alone would give the kiss of death to the whole venture. Heaven forbid they connect her with the shop here. We'd be finished."

"The coroner said he died from malnutrition not from his wounds, as you well know. I think we should at least entertain the idea. Mabel could make a batch and test it with our regular customers. Get their feedback. Then, we put it in pretty little tins and start selling it nationwide. Just like Quimby."

Charles sucked his tongue over his upper teeth as he considered the fanciful scheme. An effective medicine with low-cost ingredients might be the answer. Except he didn't want to rely on the girl for anything, not sharing his son's faith in her at all.

Mabel looked up at the ceiling that night, hearing the footsteps of the two men as they paced around their rooms, pondering their future. Archie was planning to buttonhole his network of friends to fund the initial production run. Charles considered Mabel's track record. The woman was neither a business owner nor a druggist. The idea of her unlocking their full financial potential was preposterous. What was Archie thinking?

Charles wanted to topple Quimby off his perch and was determined to find a different way to engineer his downfall.

*

On the sabbath, Archie walked with Mabel to All Saints' church, its buttery-white spire towering above the sunlit common. It was the first time that Archie and Mabel had been alone together for quite a while.

"It's a shame father is feeling off-colour today and can't come with us."

"Maybe for you. It's a blessing for me. He still hates me."

"He's having trouble adjusting, that's all. I do wish he would stop criticising your efforts. Someone had to step into my mother's shoes and help us. I have no idea when she will be back. Still, I have thought of a way that we could win him over. Since my plan to feed him into submission has failed, the next best way to charm him must be through his wallet."

"I don't understand."

"Yes, you do. It was your idea. Mail order!"

"Go on," said Mabel.

"First, I need you to tell me what's in your ointment."

As they walked, Mabel wracked her brains to remember what she and Mrs Kirkham had used and the all-important ratios.

Back at the shop, Charles was in fine fettle, lost in his own little world, thinking about retribution. A gloved hand made a soft knock on the glass door. A young woman beckoned to come inside.

"We're closed today," barked the father, not even bothering to look up.

The woman knocked again. She was not used to taking no for an answer.

"I'm terribly sorry, Mr Stanford, but it is an emergency. My father is struggling with his digestion. I need you to give him something for the pain."

"Why didn't you say that earlier? Anything for my friend Anthony Ashley."

Seizing the opportunity to impress one of Blackheath's most affluent men, Charles set to work—not only on the remedy but also a matchmaking plan for his son and the woman in front of him, young Georgina. That knock at the door felt like the answer to his money worries had tumbled into his lap from heaven.

"Can I get you a cup of tea while you wait? The kettle is hot."

"Thank you, Mr Stanford. Will it take long to prepare the prescription? I don't have much time."

"It'll be done in a flash. I think I should come back with you, just to double-check it's nothing serious. You can't be too careful with abdominal pain."

"Marvellous, Mr Stanford. So many people in this life are a let-down. You're a breath of fresh air. It's such a relief to know you will help us."

"I will be fastidious with his aftercare, my dear," he beamed, mainly because the visits would give him time to suggest that Archie would make an excellent son-in-law.

*

The next morning over breakfast, Charles was quibbling about Quimby's continued assault on the nation.

"I still think we should buy some of his things, father. Find out what it's like to place and order and receive the goods?"

"Over my dead body! I'm not giving that swindler a penny."

"But surely, the more we know about him and his operation, how well he fulfils the orders, the easier it will be to compete against him? There's no point reinventing the wheel, is there?"

"I repeat! He's not getting a penny from me."

"Alright, I'll respect your wishes, father. But I don't agree with you!"

Mabel could hold her tongue no longer. She pointed to Quimby's advert in the paper and several other questionable cures and health-giving gizmos peppered throughout the publication.

"I hope you don't feel I'm speaking out of turn, Mr Stanford, but I think we could make headway with the mail-order idea. Railway lines criss-cross the country, opening up all the industrial cities to us. We don't have to be limited to Blackheath. There is nothing special about Cornelius other than he has lots of swagger. His wares are not a proper cure."

Charles stirred his porridge, doing his best to ignore Mabel. She tried again.

"I think with an effective treatment and eye-catching packaging, we could knock Quimby into a cocked hat. When I lived with my parents, I learned how to make fancy boxes. We could soon rustle something up that would look fantastic."

Despite spending most of the past few days mulling his own mail-order line, Charles berated her. His outburst reminded Mabel of one of her father's petulant tizzies. All noise and spittle with not a lot of reason. It made her more determined to bring the idea to life, with or without the credibility that Charles Stanford might add to the product.

"I've never heard anything so preposterous in all my life. I will not tarnish my name by entering such a fraudulent business. Quimby's cures are nothing but sugar pills. They do nothing for the patient. I suggest you get on with the cleaning. Rather than advising me on how to run my business. I think you need to learn your place."

"I do apologise. Mr Stanford," she said before scurrying off to sweep the shop.

"Why are you so stubborn, father? I think it's a good suggestion. What harm can it do to try? Perhaps we could get someone to invest in the operation? That would get us going?"

"I think you need to learn your place too, my boy. We might as well tell all, and sundry our coffers are bare. Have you no shame?"

Charles barged past his son, grabbed his apron from the back of the door and lumbered downstairs to open the shop. Left alone, Mabel continued the conversation.

"If we go ahead, Archie, a couple of things need resolving: it looked and smelled rather awful!"

"But don't they say the worse a medicine tastes, the more it works?" Archie joked. "I'm willing to try if you are? We must do something to keep the pharmacy afloat for my father. If Quimby can sell hundreds of thousands of packets of his stuff, surely we can sell one thousand of ours?"

"But how will we afford the materials? And the newspaper advertising? I have no money, and neither does you—or your father, not that he would give it to us."

"Don't worry. Leave that to me," said Archie. "I have a plan."

19

GROVELLING VISITS

"Thank you for agreeing to see me, Simeon."

"My pleasure, dear fellow. Mr Emsworth mentioned that he was worried what might happen to your father's business—"

Douglas's voice trailed off.

"Yes. Losing that large workhouse contract has become a concern for us."

"There has been a lot of upheaval in the infirmary. Not to mention the unfortunate business of Miss Nithercott caught in the crossfire of Pickering's sudden appointment. It appears she vanished one day, and nobody in the workhouse knows where! Mr Emsworth is concerned. Although, there is a slight plus. Her absence has caused a few problems for Pickering."

"What a shame! That couldn't happen to a nicer chap," Archie added wryly. "And—err, I can help you with Mabel's whereabouts, reverend."

Bennett raised his eyebrows.

"She assists my father at the pharmacy. Well, she's helping around the house whilst my mother is away dealing with a family matter. However, we intend for her to work with customers when the shop is busy. As you know, she has a healthcare talent.

"Indeed, she does," said Simeon. "Now, you mentioned you needed my help. What can I do for you, old chap?"

"You might remember that Miss Nithercott had been working on an ointment with Sister Beresford. For skin complaints."

"Go on—"

"Well, you may have noticed in the newspapers that many cures are now available through mail order. So, we thought that it was worth marketing Mabel's balm to a wider audience."

"I agree," said Simeon. "But how can I help with that?"

"If we are to compete with the likes of Quimby, we are going to need money for stock and advertising. But, based on the trials in the infirmary, we are confident that the balm is effective and can be made in sufficient volume at my father's pharmacy. Its ingredients, from the hedgerows, mainly witch hazel, are cheap to gather and will give us a reasonable profit margin. But my father doesn't have enough money to cover the expense of sales and marketing."

"And?" said the reverend.

"Well—" said Archie squirming, "—I was hoping that Tynedale Hall would invest in our operation. I know you help local businesses. For example, you assist carpenters in need of replacement tools if their set is stolen. By giving us this opportunity, my father will be able to keep the chemist's open and help more people be free from disease, locally and nationally. And I'm sure you'll appreciate stopping Cornelius from conning people, just like Jesus protected pilgrims from the moneylenders and thieves in the temple."

"Well, it's a strange request, Archie, "I must say--"

"But it's an important one," the young man pleaded.

"This investment you are seeking? How much money are we talking about?"

"We estimate we'll need ten pounds for the ingredients and another hundred pounds for postage, packing and advertising. We hope to be self-funded once the first batch has been sold, though."

"Why didn't he come here to ask himself, Alastair? What made him send you?"

"Well, he's very busy, and because he knows I'm in the area as I have my delivery round--he thought it best that I pop in—."

"Did he now?" Simeon interrupted, aware that he was being spun a yarn, albeit for noble reasons.

Archie gave a faint smile and a nod.

"Alright, wait here, I need to talk to the treasurer, see how bare our cupboard is. The cost of housing all these Cambridge undergraduates is exorbitant at the moment. They always want to come during the summer break."

"Thank you, reverend. We will pay back the loan as soon as we can." grovelled Archie. "I—we—do appreciate it."

Left alone, the ambitious young man stood up and paced around the room, hands in his pockets, wondering what the outcome would be. Then, when he heard the distinctive shuffle of the cleric's soft shoes coming back, he scuttled back to his chair and sat down bolt upright, hoping that made his body language appear 'confident'.

"You're in luck, Archie. The treasurer has taken pity on your endeavours. I believe Miss

Coutts has sent us yet another donation to keep us afloat. She really is an angel. However, he wants to make sure that the hall does not take on unnecessary risks. Therefore, he will not pay a penny towards advertising until the stock is manufactured. That's his best offer."

He gave Alastair a wry grin as he handed some money over.

"Your father has helped this parish a lot, and it is comforting to know that I've been able to return the favour--even if he knows nothing about it."

"Thank you, reverend. We'll get the first batch made up this weekend," said the young man, hoping that he hadn't lied to the cleric for a second time that day.

*

The next port of call for Alister was Lydia Kirkham's front room. Mabel said there was a good chance she would be there as she seldom got out these days. His cart trundled up Dean Street. He tied up Toby and hoped the horse would be there on his return. To improve his odds, he spoke to Bert, the rag man who stood beside his mountain of stock and asked him to watch the beast.

"I'll give you tuppence, now--"

"Thank you, squire."

"--and tuppence if he's still here when I get back. Deal?"

Bert nodded. Archie hurried down Prospect Street, looking for number four. He peered through the lone grimy window pane and saw an old woman sitting, embroidering, in a rocking chair. He knocked on the door and put on his best smile.

"Mrs Kirkham, Mrs Lydia Kirkham?" he enquired.

"Who's asking?"

"I'm Archie Stanford. I believe Mabel Nithercott used to live next door."

"She's the person who sent me to see you, is she?" Lydia said suspiciously. "You'd better come in. My son's due back any time, so no funny business."

"I promise my motives for visiting are honourable, Mrs Kirkham."

Archie doffed his cap and stooped to enter the tiny front room.

"You'd better take a seat. All bent up like that."

Archie explained Mabel's plan, and the old woman's beaming smile shone out from her face brighter than the glow from a lighthouse.

"Of course, I'll help. That girl has had nothing but bad luck recently. The poor thing needs a break."

Archie gave a sigh of relief.

"So, young man, we will go to Essex this weekend and get the raw materials. The rest we can pick up from Exmouth Market, simple things like paraffin wax. You'll have to pay for it, mind. Me and Harry haven't got two ha'pennies to rub together. His wages seem to go nowhere these days."

"Thank you, Mrs Kirkham. I'll bring Mabel here tomorrow."

The old woman's heart glowed at the thought of being reunited with the girl once more.

*

The next day, Archie set off on his rounds early. He argued with his father, who was determined to ensure the girl had another day of drudgery.

"She is going to Smithfield to buy some cans of that Argentinian corned beef. It's the only way we'll be able to afford any meat for the rest of the month. Unless you have a better idea?"

Given they had eaten bread and jam a lot recently, Charles had no option but to relent.

The trio had collected everything they needed by late afternoon and then began brewing a big batch of the mixture in Lydia's kitchen. In such a cramped space, the process was fraught.

"Can't you be careful, Mabel?"

"The pan's so small, I can't help but spill some as I stir. It was fine for five portions. It's not built for five hundred."

"We'll be here all night at this rate," complained Archie, looking at the heap of ingredients yet to be processed.

There was a knock at the door.

"Argh. Who's that!" groaned Mabel as Lydia lurched towards the door.

"Good evening, Mr Emsworth. And what brings you here? We are a little busy now."

"I thought you could use this? Reverend Bennett wanted to lend it to you."

Douglas swung a large catering-sized saucepan from the hall in front of him, then placed it on the table. It was enormous, big enough to bathe a toddler in, thought Archie.

"Fabulous!" cheered Mabel as she decanted the brew into the bigger bowl.

"Simeon's told me he's got some old five-gallon cooking oil cans. He says you're welcome to those too? Maybe you can use them for storage?"

The trio could not believe their luck and thanked Douglas as he bounded off to the hall like a boomerang to collect them. On his return, the cooking process was complete, and it was time to decant the mixture from the massive pan. With a very steady hand, Mabel began ladling the mixture into the cans.

"It's not much to look at, Mabel? A bit runny, isn't it?" said Mr Emsworth.

"Don't worry. The paraffin wax will thicken as it cools but still be the right consistency to rub on. We're going to add a little fragrance and some colouring back at the pharmacy. We'll need to experiment with that, so we didn't want to add it now and make a mistake."

"It will go from this beige gloop to a wonderful smelling pinkish delight. Hopefully," added Archie.

"Thank you so much for letting us make it here, Lydia," said Mabel.

"Just remember me when those sales start rolling in. I could do with a new rocking chair. This one creaks terribly."

Mable and Archie returned to the pharmacy in the moonlight, with Toby, the ever-faithful carthorse, plodding on ahead. It had been a twelve-hour day of solid graft, and they could barely sit upright on the driver's seat. It would be well past supper by the time they got back. Charles was going to be livid.

"Where should we hide these cans?" asked Mabel.

"Let's leave them out here under the tarp. Should be safe enough. I'll check on my father. Later, when he's asleep, we'll sneak it into the coal store. He never goes out there. You wait here a minute."

Archie went to see one of the street sellers with a rumbling stomach and got three steaming hot jacket potatoes for their evening meal. When they got upstairs. Charles was fast asleep in his favourite chair by the fire, the newspaper slowly sliding down his lap.

"That's a good sign. He might retire to bed soon?" whispered Archie.

Softly, he shook his father by the shoulder.

"Got you some food, Pa."

"Where on earth have you been all day?" Charles snapped.

"I got tied up with the deliveries. The coster-mongers were everywhere, clogging up the roads. So, I ended up doing a lot on foot. Mabel watched the cart whilst I was gone. It's a good job she was there."

His father looked unconvinced. Mable served up the meal putting extra butter on Charles's potato.

He grunted in thanks as she set down his plate.

Once again, the meal was eaten in silence. Charles suspected that Archie was up to something but couldn't quite put his finger on what.

"I think I'll turn in," said Charles. "One of my regulars lent a book to me, 'The Mayor of Casterbridge'. I'll treat myself to a nice read and a cup of tea in bed."

"I'll make a brew for you," said Mabel, leaving her potato half-finished.

"No need," said Charles tersely.

He poured the hot water onto some tea that he'd used earlier, then retired, the book tucked under his arm. Alister and Mabel weren't sure if there was no noise coming from his bedroom because he was asleep or because he was reading, so they waited until gone midnight before they went downstairs and started experimenting with the balm.

Archie sneaked in one of the canisters from the yard, and Mabel decanted a small amount into an empty gripe water bottle.

Back in the shop, working by Mabel's oil lamp turned up to its brightest setting, they began creating their final prototype. It proved tricky to get the consistency and colour just right. Over the next few evenings, when Charles was safely tucked up in bed, they refined the mixture several times until Mabel was happy with its fragrance, colour, and viscosity. Archie thought she was fussing too much, but she was adamant.

"We don't want it oozing out of the tins if it gets warm in transit, do we?"

"I suppose not."

The oversight had annoyed Mabel. Archie had gone off and secured a gross of tins with loose-fitting lids rather than tubs with screw-on caps. He had thought he was doing the right thing, getting a good deal from one of the reverend's congregation, a sheet metal worker who came forward to help. Instead, he had ended up creating an avoidable problem. Still, another one of the reverend's parishioners made the pretty labels for the cardboard boxes, which had been a win. The eye-catching design read:

"Stanford's Soothing Antiseptic Balm."

Mabel stayed up until dawn, applying a sticker to each newly folded box, panicking that time was running out, and Charles would catch her in the act. The workbench looked more like a warehouse with boxes piled up everywhere. Archie salvaged a tea chest and carefully filled it with the merchandise. As

Mabel made her unused bed look slept in, Alastair hid the chest outside, covering it up with a tarpaulin. It looked like rain was due at any moment.

"I'll take the samples to Reverend Bennett later today and show him that we have up-held our half of the bargain. We'll need to get the adverts placed soon."

"Your father wants me to scrub all the floors and the pavement outside the shop. I'll pon-der the wording at the same time. It will be a welcome distraction."

"Good idea," said Allister. "Can you write them down when you get the chance? Then I'll pop along to the Blackheath Courier and ask about running our advert."

"Should we really run it in Blackheath? If we want to keep it secret?" warned Mabel.

"Father has to find out at some point. I'm not sure I've got the strength to keep it hidden from him much longer. The thought of mak-ing more batches in the wee small hours of the morning isn't good for my constitution," he joked.

The question was, how would Charles react?

19

TRIUMPHAL ARRIVALS

A few days later, in the warm afternoon sun, Quimby and his entourage made their way into town, dressed in tribal African loincloths and headdresses. Cornelius took on the appearance of a strangely benevolent witch doctor. His gilded carriage was pulled by four snow-white Percheron horses, their manes braided and plaited with matching golden ribbons, their steady, rhythmic gait heralding his arrival.

On the roof of the carriage, a small band played the latest music-hall ditties with gusto. The sight was as unusual as it was eye-catching. Hundreds of people gathered along the road to process behind the rolling chariot, leading them like well-targeted arrows to the bullseye of Quimby's spectacle, Blackheath Common. The audience was a mix of the intrigued middle-class and desperate working-class people hoping to see the miracle worker work his magic and get their injured brethren back to work.

The educated and well-to-do audience members were harsh critics of the ringleader, whispering about 'how easily the working class could be duped by a man brimming with bravado but not brains.' For Quimby, the confidence was not vanity or pride but a genuine belief that he was a worthy man. The harsh words directed at him bounced off like an arrow off a shield. Once in position, the band continued to play as the joyous throng sang along. There was a carnival atmosphere. Quimby turned to the band at the end of the tune and made a brusque slitting gesture across his throat, and the musicians piped down. A hush fell across the common.

Cornelious clambered to the front of his vehicle and addressed the crowd.

> "Ladies and gentlemen, I stand here before you to drive away disease."

Around forty years old, Quimby cut an impressive figure, clean-shaven face, piercing blue eyes, and a squared chin, all indicative of his deep resolve and willpower. He had a commanding presence, rare elocutionary power, and his oratory was that of a well-educated man. Yet like a working-class trade union leader or titillating music hall act, he could whip up a blue-collar crowd into a frenzy too.

His main carriage took its place in the dead centre of the common. Six support vehicles flanked it to form a crescent behind.

> "People of Blackheath, I am here to free you of your ailments, rid you of disease, give you

back your health, and I will do it here live. Permit me to briefly set up my consultation area. Gentlemen!"

He snapped his fingers, the band struck up again, and a group of carpenters jumped out of the wagons and assembled a raised platform in minutes. Mabel pushed her way to the front and thought she saw Harry Kirkham fitting the handrails. Like the one at Gravesend that the newspaper reported on, the local crowd looked on at the spectacle, mesmerised, wondering what might happen next.

Quimby jumped from his chariot and strode to the front of the newly-formed platform.

"I know within this crowd, there are people who need my help. Make no mistake, for me, there is no distinction of class. The millionaire will be treated the same as the poor man—."

He paused suddenly then looked at his feet.

"No, forgive me. I have told you a lie."

Charles nudged Archie and smirked.

"The millionaire will not be treated exactly the same as the poor man. For if two men present themselves, suffering from pain, one rich and one poor, I will take the poor man first."

As the crowd cheered, he raised his hands in triumph.

"For is it not true that the poor man is a busy bee in the hive of life and all such men should be busy bees? Those with wealth sit behind a desk. Pain, disability, and discomfort is much easier for them. In life, there is no room for drones, only workers. And I believe that the man who does not work should not eat. Nothing is free in this life. Shirkers are the devil's lazy workers."

Charles and Archie looked at each other in exasperation. In the distance, Mabel thought she saw Lydia Kirkham, now accompanied by Harry. She planned to talk to her after the live demonstration.

"As you can see, I am a man who works tirelessly to help others. I do not rest on my laurels. I travel the length and breadth of the British Isles, Europe, and the New World to cure the sick. This afternoon, I'm looking for some poor urchin, some poor suffering man, and I will help him before your very eyes."

"What about the women," piped up a voice.

"I will not rub ladies--"

The crowd tittered.

"--for it is not decent."

He pointed towards a miserable looking woman in an over-the-top ostrich feather hat.

"That lady over there wants to be rubbed, I can tell."

He paused to allow the renewed laughter to peter out.

"But I think it will be very improper for me to rub ladies here in public. And besides, I must apply my rules fairly. The poor labourer cannot afford to suffer, for the fairer sex does not work at the forge or the coal face, but in more gentle pursuits like mangling and seamstressing."

There was much agreement from the crowd.

"There are many who doubt my remedies—"

Charles felt his whole body flinch at the next words.

"—but as you have seen from the eye-witness reports, here are countless testimonials of people who have benefited from the ingredients I have blended, not yet introduced into the wider pharmacopoeia of Europe. But the efficacy of my treatment has been proven by instances in their own midst, whether that is Newcastle, or Nuremberg, Sunderland, or Seville."

Quimby puffed out his chest and punched the air.

"People have used these remedies on themselves, else they have helped their loved ones use them. Respected fellows, clergymen and ministers of every religious denomination and gentlemen of means have acknowledged their efficacy and have testified to the goodness within. Others have witnessed the undeniable benefits and provided names of poor sufferers themselves, who they have seen healed."

He had the crowd eating out of his hand. The hysteria proved to Charles why his shop takings were diminishing, and money was flowing into Quimby's war chest. A few neatly stacked bottles of gripe water were never going to pass muster.

"There are those who call me 'charlatan', 'tricker' or 'quack'."

There was a peel of laughter.

"And that is why ladies and gentlemen, I now ask people with medical training to raise their hands, for they will be the arbiters of truth, observe my treatments and see the powerful results for themselves. I want two doctors to come up and see how my trick here is done."

The guffaws grew louder.

"Yes, you in the grey coat. Are you a physician, sir? Good. Come on up."

Quimby ignored Charles's hand, which had shot up like the main beam of a steam engine.

"Any more? If I cannot get doctors, then I want honest men."

Without being invited, Stanford elbowed his way through the throng and took his place to the left of Cornelius.

"So, you, sir, are you a medical man or honest?" Quimby joked, delighting in taking the upper hand.

"I am a pharmacist, Sir."

"Now, will you both swear in front of these good people that you are medical men?"

The two sidekicks to Quimby's act nodded.

"And you are not my stooges."

"Certainly not!" grizzled Charles, loudly.

The crowd whooped.

"I ask you now, is anyone suffering bodily and willing to come forward for examination?"

A skirmish developed and a gap formed around one gentleman. Quimby guessed he was easily of pensionable age, doubled over in pain, and relied on two walking sticks to keep him upright. Two friends supported him by the armpits.

"You, sir! I will help you."

The gent was duly assisted to the stage. The man's shrunken and bent form and his pallid face bore the hallmarks of chronic physical suffering.

"And, what is your name, sir?   Remember to speak up."

"John Conway, I live at 42, the High Street, Blackheath. I came from Kent, but I've lived in the capital for twenty years now."

"And what ails you, Sir?"

"Rheumatism," he replied. "I've been suffering all my life. Some days it is so bad, I am bedridden by it."

Charles looked at John's hands gripping onto the sticks so hard they trembled. The knuckle joints were badly inflamed, and the fingers badly contorted. His knees were so badly swollen that the man's trousers fitted so snugly around them that they were like a second skin. Quimby continued with his assessment.

"Have you sought aid from any doctor?"

"Why yes, Sir. I've tried a good many."

"And they have not cured you?

The man shook his head.

"Remember to speak up now, Mr Conway."

"No, Sir."

"Did they charge you anything for this failed service?"

"Yes. Yet nothing changed. Most days, I am in agony."

"You good people assembled here, to me this man's poor treatment is as deceitful as visiting the baker, who puts a stone in the bag, rather than a loaf! Do you agree?"

"Yes!" was the deafening response.

"So you see," cried Quimby, turning to face the audience, "medical science is not perfect. Had it been perfect, they would not have dared to take this crippled old man's money and leave him bedridden on multiple occasions. I cannot see the honesty that lies in taking this poor man's wage and giving him no equivalent benefit in return."

Charles secretly agreed with Quimby, and he did his best to hide the thought. The lines in the man's face softened as hope washed over him. Quimby returned to his patient and continued.

"There are some who will say you are a stooge. and I have paid you to come up here."

"You have not paid me a penny, Sir!"

"Indeed, I have not, for I have faith in my remedies."

There was much hilarity.

"Here are two cases in point."

Quimby picked up two photographs from a podium and held them aloft as he explained the story behind each sitter.

"Doubtless, others will say that I paid Percy Cochran of the Hornsby Ironworks in Middlesbrough, bribing him to say he was cured. Others will say that Logan James here, a New Yorker and recipient of my massage treatment, had feigned his return to full health. For that poor labourer, every time he took a breath, it felt like a butcher's knife would shoot through his rib cage. And yet, he was cured in twenty minutes. Here he is raising the anchor of a paddle steamer."

A gasp fell through the amazed crowd. Quimby passed the photos to the adjudicators.

"Of course, the doctors say this is all rubbish. But I have proof. Many doctors are happy to take a poor man's money without affecting a cure. It is they, not me, who are little more than rogues."

He returned to his patient and put his arm around his shoulder like he was a long-lost brother.

"So, ladies and gentlemen here is a case where the doctors have failed, yet I am going

to try and effect a cure—live on this stage—
and return this poor fellow to full health!"

Quimby took a brightly coloured box from the podium and showed it to the crowd.

"As you can see from the packaging, my ointment cures rheumatism and many other things. This man suffers because he has excessive uric acid in his blood, forming crystals in his joints. I must address that."

"Would you mind rolling your trousers up, Mr Conway," said Quimby.

"If this treatment kills me, will you sell my soul to the devil?" joked the man as he struggled to comply.

"I shall now apply the balm and massage it into this man's hands, knees and torso. Whilst I do so,   I think you should have a little music. People say it helps drown out the screams when I'm doing my dental work. Fiddlesticks is my response to that."

By now, the audience had been whipped into a frenzy. With a wave of Quimby's arm, the band struck up with the introduction to 'Champagne Charlie'. The crowd sang along heartily. Mabel's mind flitted back to Edward Harris in the infirmary. Quimby bellowed some instructions to his observers.

"Now, let us take the man and help him."

The invalid, the witch doctor and the two adjudicators trooped off towards Cornelius's gilded carriage. The medicine man gave a wave as he drew a tiger-skin rug across the door to screen the patient while performing his 'magic.' The band played several songs during the twenty minutes the showman said he needed to conclude the procedure.

"I'll be back in a tic," Mabel whispered to Archie. "I think I saw Lydia."

"Great. Leave me on my own when my father is hatching some plot live on stage!"

"It's only right I say hello after all her help."

She didn't mention Harry accompanying his mother as she drifted into the bustling crowd.

"Mabel, my dear! What do you make of this spectacle!" cooed Lydia.

Harry Kirkham winked at Mabel, and she felt her heart flutter as always.

"It's good that you found somewhere to stay, rather than the workhouse," he said sheepishly. "I never did have much luck finding you work at the telephone exchange, did I?"

"I suppose not, but at least you tried." said Mabel, "The hope of your help kept me going."

Given he hadn't breathed a word to anyone about her employability nor availability, heartless Harry stayed schtum and let her labour under a misapprehension. There was no mention of losing her important application letter either. His silence eventually gave him a guilty conscience, so he made a small gesture to atone for his wrongdoings.

"Are you hungry, Mabel?"

"Starving!"

"Mama, do you mind if I escort Miss Nithercott to the pie seller?" asked Harry, faking a posh accent.

"As long as you bring me one back too," Lydia censured. "I've had enough of meagre rations lately. Where those master carpenter's wages disappear week after week, Mabel is a mystery."

Harry ignored her as he squeezed the girl's arm at the elbow and teased her to follow him. It felt rather forward of him, and she liked it. He leant towards her, and his steely eyes peered into hers. His face was inches away now, the unmistakable sweet smell of alcohol on his breath.

"Mabel—"

"Yes?"

"I should have asked Ma if she minded if I gave you a kiss."

Mabel pressed her finger on his nose, squishing it, and pushing his head away.

"I might mind, Harry Kirkham! Did that occur to you?"

"Yes. But I was pretty sure you wouldn't mind at all, Miss Nithercott."

Harry winked at her again and gave the special smile that he knew delighted all the ladies. Mabel felt dizzy with affection at the sight of it. They returned with the pies, handing one to Lydia.

"Anything happened with the patient yet, ma?"

"Not yet. Just that band making that racket."

"I'd better find Archie. He's not happy his father is an adjudicator!"

Lydia gave a loud belly laugh. Harry watched the slink of the girl's hips as she walked away.

Eventually, Quimby's hand fumbled with the fixings holding the tiger rug in place, and it fell to the floor. Then, he took a proud step forward and addressed the crowd like a magnificent master of ceremonies at the music hall.

"I have tried my utmost to treat this man, and I'll let him tell you if he is cured. I promise that I have used every ounce of courage, strength, and energy that God has bestowed upon me. I believe I have succeeded. But I will leave it to you to decide. And, the adjudicators here will tell you if there is any humbug in my practices."

Mabel and Archie looked on open-mouthed, wondering how Charles was going to respond.

"It is my dream that soon my remedies will be used in every hospital in all the kingdoms of all the world. If I can make men use their legs again, get the lame to walk, cast aside their crutches, then surely it is time for the medical world to acknowledge my virtues and talents, for my cures to bless thousands of homes."

"Bring 'im out then!" shouted a heckler.

"My salesmen will visit every nook and cranny in the land, villages, towns, and cities. I will give some away to the most deserving who cannot afford to purchase my products in good faith. I will not sit down until every home has the opportunity of getting these remedies. I want to reach everybody. And that is why I come here in my witch doctor garb and gilded car. I want to capture people's hearts, fire their imaginations, and cure them all."

"Come on, Quimby, let's see 'im!" came the voice again.

Charles Stanford's heart sank as John Conway came out skipping onto the platform.

"Look, I have cured the man of his ailment of twenty years!"

Quimby danced around the chap like the Pied Piper himself.

"And these medical men have observed my methods. My medications can and will treat all types of rheumatism, including lumbago, sciatica, gout, neuralgia, liver disease, kidney pain, impure blood, and others. As the sun shines on God's green earth, my treatments not only provide relief but also a cure. You've seen Mr Conway rise, much to the surprise of everyone else who has been crippled for years. Look at him now, walking around with a sense of freedom. The same man who had limped into my carriage moments before, helpless as an infant. He's now galloping down the steps like a thoroughbred, weaving his way through the crowd!"

John Conway was moving about like a man in his twenties. It was like Quimby's carriage was more of a time machine than a treatment room. It was nothing short of a miracle.

"Gentlemen, thank you for lending us your expertise."

Charles stood to attention, looking into the far distance for fear of catching the gaze of one of the dumbfounded audience members. He had no idea how Quimby had pulled off the stunt, but he was determined to find out.

"Here, young man, come back. I want a word with you!" beckoned Cornelius.

The old chap skipped up the stairs once more and stood unaided. The crowd roared as Quimby turned his showmanship up another notch.

"So, will you go about day-by-day and tell everyone how you feel? Make them aware of this miracle cure?"

"I will," said the grateful patient as tears of gratitude dripped down his cheeks. "I will go anywhere you wish me to send me to sing your praises."

The medicine man with characteristic bravado replied gaily:

"How about you run the Epsom Derby? Your legs are stronger than a racehorse's now!"

There was a roar of hearty merriment mingled with ripples of applause.

"If you would like to purchase some of my remedies, please see my salesmen at the stalls dotted around the perimeter of the common."

Charles marched back to Archie. Instead of humiliating Quimby, he had ended up letting his professional credentials be used to boost his foe's own reputation.

"You calm your father down," Mabel whispered. "I'll see how the sellers clinch the deal."

Thankfully, Mabel didn't see another type of 'clinch' at the showground. If she had, it would have cut like a knife, sliced through her ribs—and pierced her gentle heart. Between two of Quimby's carriages, hidden away from view, Harry Kirkham was making eyes at the loose-moraled Milly Compton. His left hand cupped the nape of her neck as he kissed her passionately. Running his right hand over her wherever he wanted, Milly seemed completely at ease.

If she had seen their clinch, reality would have been like a punch in the gut. Harry's empty gestures would have made sense: offering to deliver her letter yet not, promising her the telephonist's job and failing. She would have viewed his help for what it was--hot air to get her, with luck, to comply with his lustful intentions. Instead, she was nothing to him other than the chance of a quick thrill. With Harry off the scene, her life would surely improve. She would have given up on cosy domestic bliss with the dashing boy who lived next door. Maybe she would have worked that little bit harder to make her balm a success? Perhaps the need for independence would have reignited her desire to be a nurse? But she hadn't seen, and she was pinning her hopes of living happily ever after on the wrong man.

In front of the stage, Charles stood beside Archie, bristling. He whispered a warning to his son.

"Quimby might be smiling now," hissed the father, "but I have a plan to bring him down a peg or two."

He showed Archie a stolen tub of ointment and grinned.

"I told you wouldn't pay that man a penny. It's time for us to engineer his comeuppance."

Little did Charles know that Mabel and Archie had already made a start on their small-scale, slow-burn assault on the roving medicine man.

20

FALLING FROM GRACE

Getting increasingly worried, Charles's plan to bring Quimby down was far simpler and far more immediate: torpedo his operation below the waterline with a single killer blow. And he knew just the weak spot to attack, Quimby's formulation.

Charles had finally noticed something health-related in the Blackheath Courier that was good for his blood pressure. A Mayfair woman had been gravely ill after accidentally ingesting Quimby's topical treatment rather than rubbing it in. The article mentioned the woman nearly died. Her husband, bent on revenge, took Quimby to court. Sadly, for Charles, the judge concluded: 'It was stupidity, not toxicity, that caused her terrible illness.'

Cornelius was ordered to make his instructions and packaging clearer. Other than that, he got off scot-free. It was all grist to the mill for Charles. Fuelled by increasing spite, he had spent some time analysing Cornelius's embrocation but had failed to get to the truth of its constituent parts. It appeared an expert witness had been called by the Mayfair husband, a scientist in toxicology at the University of Edinburgh. He said he had reservations about the safety of the product when he testified. Charles was curious about what those reservations might be and decided to plough the last of the family savings into hiring the man to debunk Quimby's embrocation—once and for all.

Meanwhile, unbeknownst to Mr Stanford, Archie and Mabel kept selling their balm in larger and larger quantities. Their operation was as smooth as any finely-tuned production line. The advertisements in the Evening Standard had been a success. Orders were flooding in from all over London; Reverend Bennett's hearty endorsement had lent legitimacy to the product's claims.

Each day, under the pretence of getting fresh vegetables, Mabel would visit the postmaster and collect the orders and delivery addresses, hiding a big stash of them in her shopping bag. Each night, hiding under the stairs as Charles slept, the girl would write the labels. The long hours were exhausting, particularly on the nights where she had to make up another batch of the mixture and put it in the tins. In the morning, Mrs Kirkham would receive the order details from Archie.

Soon, the operation had become too big to run from her kitchen table. Now, she was beavering away in Tynedale after Reverend Bennett had kindly lent the aspiring entrepreneurs a small cubby hole of an office. There, Lydia would make more batches as well as package the consignments and apply the labels, ready for Mr Emsworth to transport them to Mount Pleasant Post Office for dispatch.

Day after day, Archie apologised to his father that the traffic in London had been terrible of late, trying to hide the operation for as long as he could.

"I've told Mabel to arrange the meal a little later, just while things calm down."

"The Lord sometimes sends us tests, Archie, and we must meet those tests head-on."

Archie was pleased it was easy to disguise what he and Mabel were up to. Charles was delighted his plan to topple Quimby remained a secret too.

Soon, however, tensions came to a head when Charles received a visitor in the pharmacy.

"Ah, Miss Ashley, what a pleasant surprise!"

"Mr Stanford."

"I think you've been keeping a little secret from me?"

"Have I?" said Charles, suddenly feeling hot under the collar about the matrimonial discussions with her father.

"Yes. Archie has filled me in. I know every-thing."

Charles baulked at the news.

"This."

She placed a brightly coloured box on the counter with an empty tin of Stanford's Soothing Antiseptic Balm cocooned inside. It left Charles stunned, his mouth open and his expression frozen in surprise.

"It's fabulous. Archie tells me you are making it. My father swears by it for his workers. I'd like some more. I thought if I pick some up from you now, it will save on postage. These little expenses all add up."

"Indeed, it does. How many would you be looking for? A couple of tins?"

"Good grief, no. Twenty, Mr Stanford. We need twenty!"

"Leave it with me. I'll bring some over to you. Is tomorrow alright? I have a lot of—err—urgent prescriptions to prepare today."

"Fine, Mr Stanford. We have a few left on site to last us a day or two."

Finally, the penny was dropping for Charles about his son's prolonged absences and the dark circles un-der Mabel's eyes. For once, the evening meal was not eaten in silence, as he vowed to get to the bottom of the matter. As they finished another bowl of soup and crusty bread, Charles casually placed the empty tin in the centre of the dining table.

"Would one of you care to explain this?"

Mabel and Archie looked at each other in terror.

"Speak up. I want answers. Where did the money come from for this folly?"

"Reverend Bennett invested in the balm. I explained to him what Mabel and I were trying to do."

"Do?"

"Yes. We had to do something with the workhouse contract ending, or have you forgotten? You were like an ostrich about it."

"All you've done, dear boy, is make us look poor. I bet you've been going cap in hand to all our neighbours and clients, no doubt!" Charles shrieked.

"I did nothing of the sort. I negotiated a loan with Simeon. It was not a handout. What was the alternative? Lose this place?"

Charles snatched the balm and ripped it out of its pretty packaging, which infuriated Archie even more. Stanford looked at the tin and read out the embossed lettering with disdain.

"'Guaranteed to soothe the skin.' Do you
know how many different treatments you
might need for skin ailments? Does it cure
eczema, psoriasis, acne, rosacea, hives, der-
matitis?"

"Father, it soothes. It does not profess to
cure. It's a simple anti-bacterial home remedy for simple injuries, scalds, nicks,
chilblains, and the like. It was tested in the
workhouse under Sister Beresford's guidance for quite some time. It is perfectly safe."

"That girl is a curse on this household. She
has hitched our wagon to the medicine man's
train. My good name is going to be dragged
through the mud because of this!"

The words stung Mabel. All she had tried to do was
help save the curmudgeon's business.

"Don't talk rot, father. We have sold almost
one thousand boxes. We'll sell more now. We
can offer it in the pharmacy too."

"Over my dead body! You have betrayed me,
stabbed me in the back like Caesar."

"On the contrary, we have offered you a lifeline. I saw the figures in our banking book.
We are down to the last few pounds."

Charles explained the recent sizable withdrawal was
to pay for toxicological testing of Quimby's embrocation.

"Well, this is charming! It seems we are right not to trust each other," grizzled Archie. "Once the next rent payment is due, without sales of Mabel's balm to buoy up our finances, the pharmacy would be sunk. All because of you and your vendetta against Quimby. What if the tests find nothing? Plenty of people up and down the land have benefitted from his medicines. By Jove, you even witnessed Conway's transformation before your very eyes. There must be something novel in his products!"

"Strychnine or lead probably," sniped Charles.

Mr Stanford was right to say his name would be dragged through the mud. At Quimby's next gathering, there was a change to his well-oiled routine. One of the one thousand tins of Mabel's balm had ended up in Cornelius's possession. He had tried it on a few sore patches on his own skin and had been impressed with its potency. Worried, he decided to wage a little propaganda war to retain his market-leading position.

Furious, Charles read out the scathing report over another awkward breakfast.

"Medicine Man Speaks of Great Danger."

At his latest show at Clarence Park, St Albans Cornelius Quimby warned the crowd not to rely on quack cures, particularly Stanford's

Soothing Antiseptic Balm. Holding a tin aloft, he urged the public to be careful. " When I have tested this balm, there appears to have been no benefit. Worse, if the mixture gets in the eyes, perhaps after absent-mindedly rubbing the face after application, it may result in blindness. It is the type of quack cure that must be banned. I have sent a tin of the devilish brew to the London Trading Standards Office, so they can insist it is removed from sale."

Mabel was livid because of the slur to her integrity. Archie was livid at the slur to the product. Charles was livid that what was left of his professional reputation was disappearing before his eyes. But, very much against Charles's wishes, Mabel and Archie continued their endeavours a few days later.

"It's all hot air from Quimby. He's either done nothing, or trading standards have found nothing. But, nevertheless, we must continue," Archie urged the girl as he showered the table with letters from grateful customers. "These people need our help."

After a few sleepless nights pondering the consequences of Quimby's threats, Archie and Mabel vowed to carry on and plough whatever profits were left after repaying the loan back into production. Hopefully, few of their potential customers would have read Cornelius's little diatribe.

"It'll be forgotten soon enough," consoled Archie.

"At least it wasn't on the front page, like his wretched adverts," Mabel noted. "This too will pass."

21

TUMBLING FORTUNES

Unfortunately for Charles, things at the chemists only got worse. Following the roadshow, orders for pharmacy stock tumbled as more locals invested in Quimby's quack cures. Secretly, the pharmacist had applied some of the girl's balm to his own customers to soothe a burn, and they all agreed that it provided welcome relief. Much as it galled him, he had to admit that Mabel's salve appeared to have genuine merit. Even so, he couldn't see a way to compete. Making and selling small batches would never put a dent in Quimby's thousands of units sold.

Charles felt his attempt to deal with the problem had flopped, and he regretted squandering the money on the report. '*Why is hindsight the invaluable friend who always turns up too late?*' he mused. Trapped in a downward spiral, Charles's financial woes were crushing his soul. Day and night, he looked withdrawn, defeated. Finally, concerned, and irritated, Archie decided to broach the subject of his father's maudlin demeanour after dinner.

"I wish I could help, but Reverend Bennett was quite clear that he expected the loan re-payments to be our priority. Once we get all the profits from the sales, things will be eas-ier," he volunteered as he plucked up the courage to address the real elephant in the room. "One thing I don't understand is why all our savings vanished? I thought we could limp along for a year if we were careful?"

"That was before I paid for a study--"

"A study? But you've got the office already? I don't understand."

"No, a study into what Quimby has in his products."

"But why?

"To remove the threat by disgracing the man, show his medicines to be worthless."

"I bet that wasn't cheap!"

"Err, no--."

"And this study, what's it found?"

"Well, nothing. The man looking into it has gone to ground."

"You mean run off with your money. Mother is going to hit the roof when she gets back. That's if she still has a home to come back to!"

His son was right. The comment galvanised Charles into action. He decided he needed to push Anthony Ashley to marry Georgina off to Alastair before the month was out. It turned out he didn't have to wait that long. At the next boozy dinner in Wimbledon's London Scottish golf course bar, the much-discussed deal was finally struck. All that was left to do was to tell the happy couple themselves. Georgina had a reputation for being a shrew among the eligible bachelors of the area, and Anthony was glad to have finally found a suitor.

*

The new railway in Greenwich finally opened, which made the journey to Tynedale Hall much quicker. Mabel was able to work closely with Mrs Kirkham and Mr Emsworth, who worked tirelessly to grow the fledgling operation. Welcoming some time away from grimy Prospect Street, Lydia offered to help with the housework in return for the train fare, a pie and a couple of glasses of stout. The leafy suburb made a nice change. With glee, they soon covered the last loan payment and ramped up a lengthy national advertising campaign.

> "We might not be able to compete with
> Quimby on the continent yet, Mabel, but at
> least every inch of Britain is within our
> grasp. And grasp it we will!"

22

COMEUPPANCE

Mrs Stanford might still be caring for her sister, but things were looking up. With the campaign in full swing, Mabel was inundated with even more orders. More people were writing thank-you letters. The meagre profits from the first batch of ointment eventually grew into a respectable revenue stream once the loan was cleared. Archie gave Charles the money for the landlord, and with the pharmacy's immediate financial concerns resolved, the atmosphere improved. Charles eventually allowed Mabel to help him with simple inquiries, but only when the shop was busy and couldn't serve the customers himself. After much huffing and puffing, he even began swapping the gripe water display for the balm at Archie's request. Every day, more locals came into the store to buy the cream for themselves, waxing lyrical about its efficacy. Reverend Bennett stopped by on his way to open a hall in Deptford and took a few tubs for his parishioners.

> "Make sure you share the congregation's results with us, Simeon. Then, we can add the success stories to our adverts. We'll need a full page to ourselves soon," Archie joked.

"My pleasure," the reverend replied with a grin. "By the way, I think Quimby might get his comeuppance soon. One of the junior doctors staying at the hall said his father has been paid a small fortune to test Cornelius's embrocation. More painstaking than the fellow expected, apparently. The initial results were rather baffling. He's needed to ship a special machine from America to double-check his findings. On further investigation, it seems the ointment is nothing more than turpentine, whale blubber, clove oil, and a touch of lavender to try and disguise the smell."

"Oh, really," said Archie, glancing over to his father. "The papers will have a field day. We must thank that wealthy good Samaritan."

The reverend continued, unaware of the significance of the comment.

"Yes, they love this ongoing saga with Quimby. He's touring Glasgow now. Rolled up to Bishopbriggs Park on Tuesday. I am convinced the band is there to hide the screaming as the teeth are extracted for free. Folk will do anything to save a bob or two— like those people whose hands hover over my collection plate, taking out more than they put in."

Everyone in the chemist smirked. Then, the bell door clanged, and the postman appeared with a large parcel tied up with string. Recently, he had tired of fishing the wodge of orders out of his postbag and had taken to bundling them up at the Post Office. Rather out of character, Charles gave Mabel a tiny smile.

> "I think you'd better get on with those orders rather than make the evening meal tonight. I think we can afford to go wild and dine at the Green Man Tavern just this once."

Charles didn't want to dine out to celebrate her increased sales. No, he wanted an audience that would force Mabel to sit in polite silence while he broke the good news to Archie that he would soon become a married man.

Mabel gathered up some brown paper and went off to parcel up the latest orders. One by one, she wrapped, labelled, and stacked them up on her large wooden out-tray. When no one was looking, she hand wrote a note and slipped it inside one of the balm boxes, then wrapped that one in crisp white gift wrap. She glanced about to ensure she was unseen, then hid the special package in her skirt pocket.

> "I'll just drop these off, Mr Stanford. Back in a jiffy."

"You take your time, Miss Nithercott. I think the rain has driven off all the customers to-day."

She slid a mass of boxes into her bag. Clutching the heavy handles, she struggled to put up her umbrella. As she trudged into the wet street, like her father before her, she too was missing having access to a coat.

23

DANGER LURKING
WITHIN

As he made his way along a rain-soaked Blackfriars Bridge, Archie was struggling too. His challenge was to resolve a dilemma that had been troubling him for weeks. It was becoming impossible to deny he felt an attraction for Mabel. He kept pushing the thought out of his mind, but it always popped back in, like a submerged cork bobbing to the surface. There was no doubt he was impressed by her. Despite her humble start to life, she had worked resolutely to improve her lot and rise from the slums of Prospect Street. She took the death of her mother in her stride. She had turned the hell of the workhouse into an opportunity to thrive. His own mother was the only other woman who rivalled her stoicism and drive.

He thought Mabel's willingness to help, honest and hardworking demeanour and self-deprecation were all attractive qualities in a wife. Her smile was vibrant, too, always bringing cheer to the gloomiest of moments. Sometimes, he let his mind wander, imagining her gorgeous figure reclining on that mattress underneath the stairs, a thought that proved increasingly difficult to banish. He longed to confess his feelings to her but feared it would make working together awkward if he was spurned. He was glad he had managed to hold his tongue, but for how much longer?

Out of the window, Charles spotted a woman running down Blackheath High Street, seemingly hysterical. He wondered what might have upset her. The pharmacy door nearly came off its hinges as she burst in, gasping as if her lungs were on fire. The bitter wind pinned it open against the wall.

> "Calm down, my dear. Catch your breath,
> then tell me what is troubling you."

He looked outside to see if she was being chased, but there was no pursuer to be seen.

> "I feel so awful. Please help me. I can barely
> get my breath," wheezed the woman.

> "Please, my dear. Sit down."

He came from behind the counter and brought his consultation chair over to her. She flopped in it, looking as sickly as one of Fred Kemp's poor horses.

He took her pulse. It returned to normal nicely after all the exertion.

> "Here, pop this under your tongue, please."

He read the reading from the thermometer. Thirty-seven degrees centigrade.

"Well, that seems fine. It looks like you're
over the worst of it."

Despite that, Charles noticed the woman's eyes were
flitting everywhere. She seemed agitated and unable
to focus. Something was still troubling her.

"It might have been a simple panic attack.
Have you been feeling under strain lately?"

It was then that a man sneaked in through the open
doorway and tiptoed across the shop floor. He raised
his hand up. The cold steel of a crowbar glinted
faintly as the woman noticed him. She became more
distraught. Her corseted torso heaved like a black-
smith's bellows.

"Now, now. Pull yourself together—Miss?"

The woman grabbed her abdomen and bent forward,
groaning. Charles became more concerned. Meanwhile, behind the counter, the man was scouring the
shelves looking for the distinctive yellow and blue label of Sydenham's Laudanum. A-ha. There it was.

The thief went to slip it in his pocket, but in his haste,
the bottle knocked against the countertop. Charles's
head swivelled to look at the man, who looked startled. Charles noticed his eyes were dull, and his
cheeks were dark and sunken.

"You there? What the blazes do you think
you're doing?"

His woozy expression and difficulty in finding his tongue told Stanford he was dealing with an addict. The shoplifter panicked.

"Nuffin, now get out of my way, old man!"

As his temper boiled over, Charles spotted the crowbar and lunged for it. A fearsome struggle broke out between the two men.

"Stop!" yelled Mabel, just back from the Post Office.

She'd seen Fergus O'Brien deal with so many squabbling drunks at the Little Drummer Boy she knew how to handle the situation. She lurched at the robber and pushed her thumb between the two bones of his forearm for all she was worth. Eventually, the man lost control of his grip, and the crowbar tumbled to the floor. As Mabel bent down to pick it up, it was then the robber struck, smashing the bottle against the counter and plunging the jagged edge deep into Charles's thigh. The robber dropped the glass in shock as blood spurted from the severed artery. Mabel was incensed and wanted to take the thief on herself but knew stopping Charles's bleeding was more urgent.

"What have you done, Bert? Look at him. He's a goner!" said the woman, now fully restored to health.

"Shut up. Quick, let's go."

"Are you stupid? You're covered in blood,
Bert! The plod'll have our guts for garters."

Bert snatched at the woman's arm, and they fled. Overcome with shock, Charles's grip on the counter-top failed him, and he tumbled to the floor. As he clutched his leg. Mabel grabbed her apron and used the strings to make a basic tourniquet. Focused on dealing with the injury, Mabel lost sight of the thwarted robbers as they made their escape.

"Stay still, Charles! Try not to move."

His head bobbed and swayed as he struggled to look at the wound. Things looked serious indeed. Mabel ran to the doorway and yelled with all her might.

"Call the doctor now! It's Mr Stanford. He's
been attacked."

She ran to the back office and picked up a thick wad of cotton dressing pads, then pressed them on top of the wound. Charles was now too weak to manage the task alone.

"Doc's on his way, Miss. Sent my lad over for
you," a passer-by advised.

"You'll be alright, Mr Stanford. I'm here.
Don't you worry."

Mabel wished someone could give her a pep talk as the nerve-wracking wait for the doctor to arrive began.

*

Blackheath was normally a well-to-do area. Grievous bodily harm was a rare occurrence. When a policeman on the corner saw the bloodstained thief dart out of the chemist, instinctively, he ran after them. He sent his colleague back to check on the shop.

"Oh, officer! Thank goodness!" croaked Mabel.

"You keep calm, Miss. You're doing a good job there. Much better than I could."

Charles lost consciousness. Mabel slapped his cheek as firmly as she dared. His eyes opened again.

"Stay with us, Charles. The doctor has been called. Come on now, be brave. Think of your wife and Archie. They are worth holding on for."

After a couple of anxious minutes, the medic arrived. First, he checked the area around the tourniquet.

"Hmm. The blood is beginning to congeal, stemming the flow. There is still a pulse in the limb below the ligature. Well done, Miss. Your quick thinking has saved this man's life."

Mabel gave no response, the shock and the enormity of the event overcoming her.

"You should be very grateful to this woman," said the doctor loudly as he applied another thick pad of bandages above the tourniquet. "She's kept you alive, Charles. Do you hear me?"

Groggily, he nodded.

"Press the tourniquet again, please, Miss."

He rinsed his bloodied hands then fumbled in his black leather bag.

"Now, we'll give this a little longer to settle down. Ten minutes or so. Then I shall stitch the wound in the artery."

Mabel watched the doctor complete the procedure in awe.

"He's going to need to convalesce now. If he moves, he risks opening up the gash again." warned the physician.

"Don't worry, I'll look after him. I read about what to do in Honnor Morten's nursing book," said Mabel nervously.

"Well, that explains why your technique was exemplary, Miss. If he needs anything else, come and get me. Otherwise, I'll check back in a few days."

Mabel nodded and bade the doctor farewell. No sooner had she closed the door than she was startled by a voice.

"What on earth happened here?" it asked.

The newcomer stared at the scarlet splatters plastered all over the counter and the smears of it on the floor. Snowy-white glass fragments were ground into the dark floorboards.

"Alastair! I am so pleased to see you. The doctor says he needs rest now while that artery heals."

Mabel explained about the robbery at a million words a minute.

"It's a good job you were here, else heaven knows how he would have survived. What do you say, father?"

Charles nodded with silent resentment and gratitude.

"I think you owe Mabel an apology, Pa. You have been beastly to her since she arrived from the workhouse, despite everything she has done to help us keep this place. And now this."

Archie's eyes bored into his father until he complied.

It was true. He did have a debt of gratitude. At that moment, the icy chemist warmed to the girl, finally appreciating what Archie had from his first encounter.

As he lay back in his bed, Charles' mind drifted to his plan to marry off his son to the shrewish but wealthy Georgina Ashley. With a free hand to decide his future, surely Archie would choose Mabel to be his bride—especially now. He wondered if Mabel felt the same way. She was very guarded about her emotions, distant even. Was the relationship between them purely commercial? Or was there more to it? It was a difficult situation. Antony Ashley was not the type of man who would put up with any messing about. There would be serious ramifications if the marriage contract with Georgina was broken off.

*

With his enforced bed rest, Charles was trying to keep on top of his invoices and receipts. However, he found it far more enjoyable to read serialised short stories in the paper. He was particularly engrossed in one when there was a knock at the bedroom door. Thinking it would be Mabel clucking and fussing around him, he was snappy.

"What now? Is it important?"

"Yes, it is," replied the policeman. "It's Constable Ryan. May I come in?"

"Enter."

"Good afternoon, Mr Stanford. I have news of your attackers, Albert Stratton, and his side-kick, Violet Goffin. We managed to catch them as they fled towards Lewisham train station. A couple of witnesses confirmed they saw them running out of your shop. They have both been arrested and charged. It appears they have been involved in a spate of attacks in Kent that were becoming increasingly violent as Albert's addiction sped out of control."

"I am delighted they are to be brought to justice. A job well done, constable. Please keep me updated on any developments."

"We will need a proper statement from you, now you are feeling stronger."

"Of course."

The next visitor to knock at the door was Anthony Ashley, also with some good news which he shared enthusiastically after the formality of asking Charles about his health.

"I've been speaking to the vicar of All Saints church. He will read the first of the banns this month. Have you had a chance to speak to Archie yet? You said you were sure he would be amenable?"

Charles dodged answering the question by asking one of his own.

"How has Georgina taken to the idea?"

"She is delighted. For some unfathomable reason, some chaps think she is difficult, abrasive even, and finding a suitor has proved a struggle."

"Really? She is a little spirited, I agree, but that adds to her charm," Charles stalled.

Archie appeared. He saw his father, perspiring heavily, looking pale and tired.

"I think father has had a lot of visitors today," the son said as he bundled a speechless Anthony out of the room. "He needs his rest."

"Things will be different with a strong wife to share your burdens with, Archie. But I know you will be happy together," said Anthony.

Charles cringed as he overheard the exchange between the two men and panicked about how to break the marriage promise with Anthony and Georgina. Archie didn't have the faintest idea of what Ashley meant. He was busy hoping no one would not pick up on his affection for Mabel, making a point of being nothing more than civil to her in public until he had a chance to talk to confess his true feelings to her.

In the Stanford's small kitchen, Archie watched Mabel trim the vegetables for Sunday lunch.

"I've been looking at the figures. Our orders have tripled this week," she announced with a big smile. "So, I decided to treat us to a pork knuckle. They say the way to a man's heart is through his stomach, so I thought I'd try and keep on your father's good side for five minutes at least. It seems saving his life wasn't quite enough to win him over."

They both chuckled.

"I am looking forward to a good feed, Mabel. It's been such a hard week, and then the shock of the attack on my father. I—err— never did say thank you properly. You were amaz—"

Mabel blushed at the trailed off compliment.

"It is me who should be grateful. You gave me the chance to escape the workhouse when Mr Ensworth was sacked. You lent me your ear after the death of my mother. You persuaded Simeon to invest in the balm. I should be thanking you. Shall we call it quits?"

Alone, listening in on their warm conversation, Charles continued to sweat as he wondered how and when to advise Ashley that Georgina's engagement was off. Now the banns were about to be read, things were getting serious.

*

Monday morning arrived, and Archie called to Mabel.

"You'd better come here quick!"

Moving into full action stations, Mabel hurtled downstairs.

"What is it? What's wrong? Is it your father?"

"The postman needed two sacks to bring all the postal orders. You'd better help him before he collapses under the strain too."

"You tease!" she complained. "I thought it was a real crisis!"

She put the orders on the office table. They formed a deep pyramid, covering all the desk space.

"Let me help you, Mabel. I've got a bit of time before I head to Tynedale. After that, I'll speak to Sid about getting some more packaging."

Archie sniffed the air then looked at the girl wide-eyed. There was the unmistakable smell of burning toast permeating the air.

"Miss Nithercott," yelled Charles.

"Oh no! Your father's egg and soldiers. It's his favourite breakfast--"

"—when you've not cremated it?" Archie joshed.

"Thank you for your faith in my cooking skills. Haven't you got to get Toby ready?"

"Already done. I was up with the lark."

She scraped the worst of the blackened bits off the toast and brought in the tray to Charles's room. Laying down the tray, all she said was a polite 'morning' and made her way out of the room backwards. She looked like a nervous servant leaving Henry VIII's bedchamber. Usually, when she attempted a conversation early in the day, he would snap back at her. But this morning, it was different.

"Mabel. I never really did get a chance to thank you for saving me the day I was attacked. And for your help since you moved in. I've been most unkind to you when all you have done is try to help us. It's because I miss my wife, and seeing you working reminds me that she's not here. It's nothing personal. Sometimes you want life to be different, but it isn't, and that makes one irritable."

"You owe me nothing, Mr Stanford. You and Archie saved me from the workhouse, and for that, I am grateful."

Before he left for the day, Archie overheard the exchange and smiled. There was one more chance for this mess with Georgina to resolve itself for Charles. The question of Joe Nithercott. Would Mabel live with him on his release from Newgate?

"Your father, he must be out soon? Has there been any news?"

"None. It's as if I am dead to him. Lydia says because of the overcrowding problem, he was released early for good behaviour. No one knows where he is, though. Jimmy McGinty reckons he has remarried and moved away to Liverpool. So, I am living the life of an orphan. That makes your help all the sweeter."

She stopped, then reached in her pocket and gave a card to Charles.

"I believe a calling card came for you earlier. It was lying on the doormat first thing this morning." she said. "Somebody must really want to see you."

Charles looked down and read the name and blanched: Anthony Ashley.

"Can you tell him I am not up to visitors, but I will speak to him before Sunday?"

'I need to think   of something. And quick.'

24

ANOTHER SLICE
OF CAKE

A Saturday afternoon off couldn't come too soon for Archie. Mabel was exhausted, being pulled in all directions: housemaid, nursemaid and production line worker. Archie was determined to give her a break, whether she liked it or not.

"What are you up to?" she asked, hearing him clanking around in the loft.

"It's got to be here somewhere!"

"What?"

"That thingy."

"What thingy?"

"Ta-da! This one."

An arm swung round down from the hatch, holding a picnic basket. Soon it would house a selection of tasty cakes and sandwiches from Watsons, the local bakers.

"Hurry up. We're meeting Lydia and a few others at Greenwich Park at one."

Mabel grinned, untied her apron, and went to get changed into her best frock—just in case she bumped into her sweetheart Harry. That day they decided to give Toby the afternoon off and walked rather than taking the cart. They were so hungry that half the picnic was eaten before they reached the park.

"I hope Lydia has brought something!" shrieked Mabel peering down into the basket. As a manual worker, Harry had a ravenous appetite, and the last thing she wanted to do was disappoint him.

It was a lovely sunny afternoon. Reverend Bennett and Mr Emsworth had escorted Mrs Kirkham to a wooden bench under the cool shade of a chestnut tree. Deer ran freely around the grounds.

Archie managed to persuade Simeon to escort him and Mabel down Lover's Walk under the pretext of admiring the decorative fountain at its far end. They chatted as they strolled.

"I would love to come to the fair in October. I've heard they install a temporary ballroom with an orchestra, 'The Crown and Anchor'. There is dancing and singing. It sounds fabulous," chirruped Mabel, imagining dancing the night away with Harry.

Simeon took a dim view.

"These fairs have become known for unseemly behaviour by 'disorderly persons' The fair sparks behaviour that was 'offending against the best feelings of Christian morality'. I have heard some of the pensioners like to charge people for a look through their telescopes to see the lewd behaviour at the top of the hill. It's not safe for a girl like you, Miss Nithercott."

Archie smiled to himself as he saw Mabel's face tighten with silent fury. He often spotted her railing against being told what to do, making her even more endearing. If it hadn't been for her tireless drive with the mail-order project, it would have been nowhere near as successful.

Her irritation continued when Lydia Kirkham revealed Harry's forthcoming nuptials to Milly Compton as the other men went to get some ice creams.

"I'm glad they've wandered off. I didn't want to gossip in front of them. Apparently, he popped the question at Quimby's visit to Blackheath. I only found out yesterday. Kept me in the dark he did, the rascal."

"Me too," Mabel fumed to herself.

"She's a bit of a wild one, that Milly. So, they're well-matched," she added, chuckling.

As the sun began to set, the party of picnickers made their way home. Mabel was exhausted and deflated and wanted to be alone. After preparing a sandwich for Charles, she excused herself and crawled into bed for an early night.

Upstairs, Archie decided to broach the subject of marriage with his father.

"I would like to propose to Mabel, father. Well, I say I would like to—actually, I'm going to, unless you have an objection."

"I'm afraid you can't, Archie."

"Why not? You either let us marry, or we will elope. It's your choice."

"I don't like your tone," warned Charles.

"Father, I can't see who would be a better bride for me than a woman who has helped make our business profitable, has shown great compassion to those in this community, has helped countless people with her cure, and even saved your life."

"I can. Georgina Ashley."

"That harpy? You can't be serious, father? Men run a mile from her."

"I'm afraid I am. Several weeks ago, when money was very tight, I made an arrangement with Mr Ashley. It was the only way I could see we could keep a roof over our heads."

"And what if I say no?"

"The banns are due to be read a week on Sunday. The engagement promise has already been made."

"Why on earth, didn't you tell me? Why did you do this behind my back? These days, it is more usual for a son to choose who he is to marry. When I've dedicated my life to help you? You could have at least discussed the matter before entering into the agreement."

He slammed his hand on Charles's bedside drawers.

"You will have to tell Anthony it is off. The whole thing, off."

"I will try. Mr Ashley will be well within his rights to take us to court for a broken marriage promise. There will be the shame of the trail. And then there will be costs awarded."

"How much money will that cost?"

"Quite a bit. Gladys Knowles was recently awarded £10,000 in damages. But ironically, it was the editor of the Matrimonial News, Malcolm Duncan, who was sued."

Archie, not appreciating his father's attempt at levity, stormed out. Fortunately, the argument had not woken Mabel. Heaven knows what she would have made of that exchange. In the heat of the moment, Archie seized his opportunity to follow his heart, and he would deal with the consequences later. How could he have even broken a promise his father had made it secretly on his behalf?

"Mabel. Mabel, wake up, my dear," he whispered tenderly.

"What is it? I need my beauty sleep."

Archie smiled at her in the darkness.

"Did you enjoy yourself today? I did."

"Yes. It was so lovely to be out in nature and not at that wretched desk or stove."

"I meant to ask you something when we got to the fountain, but it slipped my mind, with Simeon telling you off about wanting to go to the fair."

"What were you going to ask? Hurry up and ask me, then I can get back to sleep."

Archie gulped down a big breath of air to make sure the words came out. He stroked her face with his hand as their eyes adjusted to the gloom of the little office.

"Mable Nithercott, will you marry me?"

A thousand thoughts flashed through Mabel's mind as she evaluated the impact of the next word that came out of her mouth.

"Yes. I will."

"Really!"

"Yes, now let me get some sleep!"

He kissed her lightly on the forehead.

"Let's keep it our little secret for now? Shall we?" Archie suggested with a whisper as he leant over the bannister.

Mabel nodded and gave a beaming smile.

*

Archie was dismayed to see nothing was happening with his other pseudo-engagement during his father's convalescence. Charles had not asked for a ride in the cart to Mr Ashley's home, nor had Anthony visited the shop. Naively, he hoped the whole business would fizzle out of its own accord. In the last few days, his father had been strong enough to work half-days in the pharmacy. His behaviour incensed Archie, and the young man chose to take matters into his own hands.

Frustrated by the lack of any developments, he put in an announcement of his own at his next visit to the newspaper.

"Another advert for the balm, Archie," asked the typesetter.

"Yes, and one for me."

"What would you like it to say?"

"Mr Charles Stanford is delighted to announce the engagement of his son Archie Ernest to Miss Mabel Nithercott."

"Congratulations, Archie, my good fellow! What wonderful news."

Mabel was in the back, parcelling up more orders, when Mr Ashley burst in and gave Charles a good reprimand.

"What's the meaning of this," he said, jabbing at the announcement.

"It appears your son is engaged to your housemaid! How unbecoming.

Mabel listened in on the exchange in horror.

"You and I both had a prior arrangement with Archie and Georgina. I don't need to remind you that this is a clear breach of promise, and my daughter will want significant financial compensation for the shame and hurt and inconvenience your reneging on the deal has caused."

Charles flinched as Anthony strode behind the counter, penning him in.

"I think a sum of two hundred pounds is reasonable. I had approached the vicar about the banns. That man can't keep anything to himself. It is an open secret around the village. Everyone will know she has been shunned through no fault of her own.

'Two hundred pounds!' panicked Mabel, her chin hitting the desk at the size of the sum. There was no way she and Archie could get that sort of money together.

"I think Georgina has ideas above her station, Sir. The arrangement has only been in place for a matter of weeks. Furthermore, it was a private arrangement that only you and I were aware of, not even the 'happy couple'. So, the vicar's idle gossip at the summer fete is not a matter of great concern."

Anthony Ashley was wound up like a coiled spring.

Reading the situation was about to get violent, Charles made a counteroffer after totting up the profit the balm might bring in.

"I am willing to pay you half that, in instalments of ten pounds a month. Take it or leave it. This is my final word on the matter."

"We shall see about that," said Anthony. "I'll give you one week to get the full two hundred."

Mr Ashley marched off and called a carriage to take him home. Charles wondered if the idea of being stuck with his harpy of a daughter for a little bit longer was rubbing salt into the wound. He chuckled at the thought of him getting her an army officer as a husband so she would have to accompany him on tours of duty in a far-flung war zone."

Mabel came out to see Charles, horrified that he'd have to spend two hundred pounds to avoid being sued.

"I will help you pay Charles. I cannot blame you for wanting a worthier, wealthier match for Archie than I, a girl from the Prospect Street tenements."

"That is who you were, my dear, but it is not who you are. You have proved yourself to be caring, compassionate, wily, even with this balm business of yours. My family is prospering once more thanks to your efforts. Archie has my blessing. I know that you will both be happy together and that you will make a good job of running this business when I'm gone."

"Don't talk like that," said Mabel. "You're going to be with us for a long time, and I'm going to delight in looking after you—until Mrs Stanford comes back. There won't be room for two of us here."

25

THE PARCEL

Earlier that week, a curious parcel wrapped in stiff white card had arrived at the home of Thomas Beecham. His valet had dropped it off along with that morning's copy of The Telegraph, complete with a glowing advertisement for Stanford's Soothing Balm at the top of the front page.

"Didn't you think to open it, Gerald," said Beecham. "No, it was marked private, Sir. I know how irritated you can be when I open your personal correspondence. So, I erred on the side of caution."

"Open it now, will you?"

"Certainly, sir."

It was like a pass the parcel prize. Opening the first layer of the wrapping revealed an envelope which he slid across the crisp white table. Gerald continued to unwrap the gift as Beecham left his fresh grapefruit to read the letter, curious about its contents.

"Dear Mr Beecham,

Please find enclosed a tin of Stanford's Soothing Antiseptic Balm, which I have been making at Tynedale Hall. I was wondering if you would be interested in licencing the formula from me? Unfortunately, it is becoming increasingly difficult to meet the demand from such a small facility. However, with your pharmaceutical factory in St Helen's, I am sure together we could meet the demand for my product, both nationally and hopefully internationally.

Yours sincerely,

Miss Mabel Nithercott.

Beecham knew the name instantly. Not only had she been able to save the life of a chemist who had been viciously attacked, but it appeared she was also the brains behind the cure-all ointment that people across the country were raving about.

Beecham had heard about the salve through his network that the product had come to Victoria's attention. And although it had not been used by royal appointment officially, it was clear that she believed in the product and had given tins to many of her household staff.

It was with that in mind that he decided to agree to licence the treatment from Mabel.

"Take a note for me, will you, Gerald."

"Certainly, sir."

"Dear Miss Nithercott—"

*

On immediate receipt of the letter, Mabel sent a telegram to Beecham saying they would be there the next day, her galvanizing zeal forging ahead as ever.

Mabel, Archie, and Charles took a train to Liverpool. In the morning, the trio found themselves in front of the great man himself and his son, Joseph.

Beecham slid a contract across the table for the two men to investigate. Mabel was invited to take tea in the parlour as the business negotiations took place. She looked like she was about to decline the offer. Charles was livid, thinking she might jeopardise the whole deal. He gave her a dark look, and with reluctance, she left.

Half an hour later, the two men re-emerged.

"The deal is done," said Archie.

"And?"

"He is prepared to pay as much as one penny per unit sold as a licence royalty," said Charles.

"A penny. You fool! We have to pay Ashley, and fast!" Mabel hissed.

"—and an initial payment of three hundred pounds to begin production," Charles added.

Mabel felt guilty for her lack of trust in her future father-in-law.

"There is just one thing. He wants to market the product under a new name. He expects us to receive thirty thousand pounds a year within three years."

Mabel could hardly believe her luck. The name change was an easy thing to forego to secure such a lucrative deal.

Within weeks, the cash started rolling in from the agreement with Mr Beecham and large quarter page adverts appeared in the newspaper advertising "Germosalve, the new cure for light wounds."

26

THE PREPARATIONS

It was the day before the wedding when Mabel finally met Mrs Stanford.

"I've heard so much about you, my dear."

"All good, I hope."

"I always knew the woman who stole my only son's heart was going to be wonderful."

She gazed at the beauty before her and gave her a blue necklace to wear at the ceremony.

"It's my sister's. She wanted you to wear it."

"It's lovely."

"She's sorry she can't be with you, but she says perhaps she will make one of the christenings. I am so relieved she has pulled through. It seems we have two fighters in the family."

Mabel smiled at the compliment. Then, Archie knocked loudly on his parent's bedroom door.

"I'm off to stay at the Green Man with father," he said with a grin as he peered around the entrance. "He's up for a double celebration now the study into Quimby's formulation has proved the man's a fraud. The ingredients in all their glory are being published in this week's The Lancet. So, it seems the rumours about it being 90% whale blubber were true."

"That's enough chat. You'd better get off, Archie! We were just about to sort out Mabel's dress. You don't want to see it. We've had enough bad luck for a while, I think."

"See you tomorrow, my love," he whispered, blowing her a kiss as he disappeared down the stairs.

"Right then, Mabel, let's sort out this dress."

AUTHOR'S NOTE

Cornelius Quimby is based on a real man. Few patent medicine advertising campaigns could have been as eccentric as The Sequah Medicine Company's.

Advertisement for Sequah's Oil and Prairie Flower, ca. 1890. Wellcome Library reference: GC/69.

In 1887, Yorkshireman William Henry Hartley used a long-haired Native American prairie persona to promote his products. At the time, he was described as the "Last of the Mohicans." He got his company name from a Cherokee named Sequoyah. Hartley claimed that his wonder products, Prairie Flower and Sequah's Oil, were made using traditional Native American recipes.

An almanac, The Sequah's Annual, was published as a weekly penny newspaper beginning in October 1889 and included advertisements, jokes, and short stories to help sell more products. It was successful in "explaining the 'priceless value' of his medicines."

In case there was any doubt about who Sequah was, a publication titled Sequah, Who and What is Sequah? appeared to explain the branding. The products were so successful that Sequah used the Chemist and Druggist to issue a warning to other traders who tried to imitate his products in November 1889.

Sequah's travelling show was a different type of advertisement. Sequah rode atop a horse-drawn "golden chariot" illuminated by flares, accompanied by a brass band and fellow feathered "American Indians." He wore a gold chain, a head torch, and brandished the tools of his dubious trade. With free products distributed to those who could prove their poverty, word spread quickly. The Chemist and Druggist reported in February 1890 that musicians paraded the streets of Cork liberally distributing handfuls of small silver to "the gamins," ensuring the company received a "right hearty welcome."

The show, which was staged after dark for maximum drama, toured the United Kingdom, Ireland, the West

Indies, North America, and South Africa. So-called natural products were used in demonstrations of quick tooth extraction, miraculous rheumatism massages, and even séances. Sequah became one of the most successful patent medicine businesses in Britain during the late nineteenth century as a result of these performances, which were a hit with the entertainment-loving public.

Following treatment, it was claimed that Harley's patients no longer needed "many crutches and thick sticks." After the patients had recovered, he used the crutches and sticks to create a boundary fence around his vast farm, he told a Leeds audience in November 1889. This show allegedly drew 30,000 people. The Sequah hoardings were "resplendent" when The Chemist and Druggist arrived in Glasgow for business the following year.

The Sequah shows became so popular that duplicate travelling salesmen (dubbed "Sequahs") were hired to help expand the business. There were 23 'Sequahs' in operation by 1890, when a fairground steam organ was added to the attraction. According to evidence held at the Wellcome Library in London, Peter Alexander Gordon went by the alias James Kaspar and sold Sequah's patent medicine all over the world.

The Sequah's Swan Song

Why did the Victorian's rave about the Sequah's products? Prairie Flower, described as a "blessing to suffering females," was a tonic with a kick that contained a weak alkali, a vegetable extract, and a trace of alcohol. The hot flavour was provided by a sprinkling of capsicum pepper.

Sequah's Oil was essentially a warming massage balm that contained natural camphor oil (a stimulant). It claimed to be able to cure "rheumatism, liver complaints, indigestion, and all blood diseases." Both products were said to be "as certain to cure as the summer sun will melt ice."

Sequah's products had been exposed as quackery by 1897. Prairie Flower's botanic extract was discovered to have originated in the West and East Indies, not North America. Similarly, there was nothing novel in the pharmaceutical administration of the 'aloes' used in his products. Sequah oil's "fishy" reputation was confirmed when the base oil was revealed to be a cheap fish oil (apparently whale) mixed with turpentine and camphor.

There was also a deceptive reason for the accompanying drum and brass bands at the medicine shows: the music drowned out the cries of pain from those foolish enough to step forward to have their teeth extracted.

The practise of selling patent medicines in this manner has been declared illegal by the UK government. With sales of the Prairie Flower remedy peaking at 1.49 million, the company was investigated by the Inland Revenue for stamp duty in 1890. The company was dissolved on March 26, 1909, after it went into liquidation in 1895.

ABOUT THE AUTHOR

I live with my cat, Ralph, in Somerset. I love finding real stories and turning them into romance sagas. There are so many fascinating people and places to weave into an interesting tale. It's a real privilege to write them.

You can follow me on my Amazon author page, or find out more on my website. I love to hear from my readers.

Thank you for all your support.

Beryl

www.berylwhite.co.uk

Printed in Great Britain
by Amazon